There Once Lived a Woman Who Tried to Kill Her Neighbor's Baby

WINNER OF THE 2010 WORLD FANTASY AWARD FOR BEST COLLECTION

LUDMILLA PETRUSHEVSKAYA was born in 1938 in Moscow, where she still lives. She is the author of more than fifteen collections of prose, including the short novel *The Time: Night*, shortlisted for the Russian Booker Prize in 1992, and *Svoi Krug*, a modern classic about the 1980s Soviet intelligentsia. The progenitor of the women's fiction movement in modern Russian letters, she is also a playwright whose work has been staged by leading theater companies all over the world. In 2002 she received Russia's most prestigious prize, The Triumph, for lifetime achievement.

KEITH GESSEN is the author of *All the Sad Young Literary Men* and an editor and founder of the literary magazine *n+1*. He has written about Russian literature for *The New Yorker* and *The New York Review of Books*. In 2005 his translation of *Voices from Chernobyl* won the National Book Critics Circle Award for Nonfiction.

ANNA SUMMERS holds a doctorate in Slavic literature from Harvard. She lives in Cambridge, Massachusetts.

ACCLAIM FOR

There Once Lived a Woman Who Tried to Kill Her Neighbor's Baby

"[Petrushevskaya] is hailed as one of Russia's best living writers. This slim volume shows why.... Every one of the 19 stories ... presents an arresting parable.... Gessen and Summers have chosen shrewdly. In these beautifully translated pages, they deliver savory tastes of Petrushevskaya's dark perspective.... We are left hungry for more."
—*The New York Times Book Review*

"The most attention-grabbing title of the year ... Undeniably seductive."
—*More*

There Once Lived a Woman Who Tried to Kill Her Neighbor's Baby

✝

SCARY FAIRY TALES

LUDMILLA PETRUSHEVSKAYA

Selected and Translated with an Introduction by

Keith Gessen *and* **Anna Summers**

PENGUIN BOOKS

PENGUIN BOOKS

Published by the Penguin Group

Penguin Group (USA) Inc., 375 Hudson Street, New York, New York 10014, U.S.A. •
Penguin Group (Canada), 90 Eglinton Avenue East, Suite 700, Toronto, Ontario,
Canada M4P 2Y3 (a division of Pearson Penguin Canada Inc.) • Penguin Books
Ltd, 80 Strand, London WC2R 0RL, England • Penguin Ireland, 25 St Stephen's
Green, Dublin 2, Ireland (a division of Penguin Books Ltd) • Penguin Group
(Australia), 250 Camberwell Road, Camberwell, Victoria 3124, Australia (a division of
Pearson Australia Group Pty Ltd) • Penguin Books India Pvt Ltd, 11 Community
Centre, Panchsheel Park, New Delhi – 110 017, India • Penguin Group (NZ),
67 Apollo Drive, Rosedale, North Shore 0632, New Zealand (a division of Pearson
New Zealand Ltd) • Penguin Books (South Africa) (Pty) Ltd, 24 Sturdee Avenue,
Rosebank, Johannesburg 2196, South Africa

Penguin Books Ltd, Registered Offices:
80 Strand, London WC2R 0RL, England

First published in Penguin Books 2009

"Father" and "Two Kingdoms" first appeared in *n+1;* "The Arm,"
"Incident at Sokolniki," and "A Mother's Farewell" in *Vice*;
and "The Fountain House" in *The New Yorker*.

The stories in this collection were published in Russian in *Novy Mir, Ogonyok,
Literaturnaya Gazeta* and other periodicals.

ISBN 978-0-14-311466-6
CIP data available

Printed in the United States of America
Set in Minion with DuChirico Display • Designed by Elke Sigal

· Contents ·

Requiems

Fairy Tales

· Introduction ·

IN ONE OF THE SHORT MEMOIRS SHE'S WRITTEN OVER THE
years, Ludmilla Petrushevskaya described a trip she took to
Lithuania in 1973. Though part of the USSR, Lithuania was
a troublesome republic—wealthier and more European than
the rest of the empire, it was not a place a troublesome Soviet
writer could go on official business. But Petrushevskaya
wanted to make a pilgrimage to Thomas Mann's summer
home (on the Baltic coast) and also meet with a literary editor, who might not know—Vilnius was far from Moscow—
that her writing was banned in Russia. She invented a reason
to visit a Russian city near the border, then hitchhiked the
rest of the way. The year before, Petrushevskaya's first husband had died at the age of thirty-two after a long illness; for
the last six years of his life he was paralyzed.

The trip as she describes it is trying, difficult, exhila-
rating—but most of all it is a break. Wandering the early
morning streets of Vilnius, she meets a woman named Yadviga, who takes her in. The women exchange stories. Yadviga
is also a widow: She moved to the capital because her house

had burned down while she was out one morning, while her daughter, a grandson, and her husband remained inside. In return, Petrushevskaya tells the widow about her husband. At the end of his life, he was so thin he looked like Jesus Christ on the cross. They cry together. Then it's time to go. "I take the tram out of town until I reach the highway," Petrushevskaya's memoir concludes. "There's not enough money for a train. Freedom. A deafening freedom after six years of hospitals and steady fighting. Ten more days of freedom before I return to my everyday life, hold in my arms my child, my savior, my treasure. Yadviga remains alone, the dry branch of a burned tree." A month later, the Lithuanian editor sends her the handsome sum of thirty-two rubles and the Lithuanian women's magazine where two of Petrushevskaya's stories had appeared in translation.

In official Soviet literature, Petrushevskaya would remain out of favor for years to come. Her stories about the lives of Russian women were too dark, too direct, and too forbidding. Even her fairy tales seemed to have an edge of despair to them. ("Who's Afraid of Ludmilla Petrushevskaya?" was the title of a 1984 essay in an emigre literary journal which asked in part why an author who was so far from explicitly political themes should be banned.) The same editor who first published Solzhenitsyn in the Soviet Union in *Novy Mir* in the early 1960s met with Petrushevskaya in 1968 to tell her that, in her case, there was no hope. She did, however, write plays, and these fared better—one of her most radical plays, *Love*, comparable in style and spirit to Harold Pinter's early work, premiered at the Taganka Theater in 1974—but often these productions too were shut down. Petrushevskaya scraped by with television and radio scripts, occasional journalism, editing, and translations.

Finally, the Soviet Union began to fall apart. A group of writers who had never been allowed in print before began to be published in earnest, with large circulations. "The New Robinson Crusoes," one of Petrushevskaya's most famous stories (included in this collection), was published in *Novy Mir* alongside Solzhenitsyn's *Gulag Archipelago*. The appearance in 1987 of her first collection, *Immortal Love*, which gathered her grim, realist tales of Soviet life, many of them in the form of acidic female monologues, was a major cultural event. Petrushevskaya was then forty-nine. From that point on, she was officially a major figure in Russian letters, unrivaled in the scope and diversity of her talent. She has won numerous awards and her stories have entered university curricula in Russia and in the West. Her seventieth birthday in 2008 was a government-sponsored celebration on a national scale. With the death of Solzhenitsyn, it would not be an exaggeration to say that Petrushevskaya is Russia's best-known living writer.

She is still also a very controversial one: Many Russian readers cannot forgive the unremitting bleakness (even if it was always mixed with profound sympathy and hope) of her early work; others cannot accept that a writer who has existed so far outside the ordinary conventions of literary life—who once produced a nearly epic-length poem called *Karamzin* satirizing Karamzin's 1804 story "Poor Liza"; and who has recently been performing a one-woman cabaret while wearing an enormous hat—has achieved classic stature. The one expression that unquestionably fits her, a Russian critic wrote recently in *Novy Mir*, is an English one: "larger than life."

This collection represents a selection from one vital side of Petrushevskaya's oeuvre: Her mystical and fantastical tales. They are organized into four sections according to the cycles in which Petrushevskaya has arranged them in her Russian books. "Songs of the Eastern Slavs"—dark, surreal vignettes told in the manner of urban folk tales; "Allegories," including two apocalyptic stories, some of Petrushevskaya's best known, about the collapse of a social-political order; "Requiems," an older and gentler cycle that explores human relationships under duress and after death; and, finally, "Fairy Tales"—or "real fairy tales," as Petrushevskaya calls them. From over a hundred stories we chose pieces with a common fantastic or mystical element, leaving for future translations Petrushevskaya's early realistic stories; her central masterpiece, the novel *Time Night*; and her novellas and dramatic writings. The stories in this volume were composed over the last thirty-plus years, but many of them are from the past decade. Most of them have never appeared in English.

The cycles are written in very different keys, making them difficult to classify, but a subtitle Petrushevskaya used for one of her longer fantastic tales, "The Possibilities of Menippea," points to a common source. The ancient Greek Menippus once visited Hades, and since then the satirical genre named after him has often been said to include visits to the literal or social underworld. These visits are called *nekyia*, a night journey, after Homer's term in the *Odyssey*. Classic *nekyia* describe travels to the underworld and dialogues with the dead (in the original *nekyia*, Odysseus drinks human blood so as to talk with the dead); modern *nekyia*, like *Alice in Wonderland* and "The Turn of the Screw," involve extraordinary situations like near-death experiences and borderline states. Time functions differently in these tales: travels to the underworld and other parallel realities occur outside past, present, and future and may only last a few earthly seconds, like Alice's dream.

In this collection, nearly every story is a form of *nekyia*. Characters depart from physical reality under exceptional circumstances: during a heart attack, childbirth, a major psychological shock, a suicide attempt, a car accident. Under tremendous duress, they become propelled into a parallel universe, where they undergo experiences that can only be described allegorically, in the form of a parable or fairy tale. In one of her collections, Petrushevskaya invented a name for this secondary reality: "Orchards of Unusual Possibilities." Most of the action in the stories collected here takes place in the Orchards of Unusual Possibilities. Characters find themselves in a strange place without any memory of the accident that brought them there. A middle-aged Russian man wakes up in a mental hospital in New York. Another character finds himself walking alone through the winter woods at night, searching for a child he's never seen. A girl discovers that she is standing on the side of a dark road, wearing strange clothes, without any knowledge of herself. What happens to these characters on their journey in a strange land may be read as a dream, a nightmare caused by shock, or else as a momentous mystical transgression—Petrushevskaya makes a point of leaving room for both interpretations. In "The Fountain House," the father of a killed girl falls asleep in the hospital, and in his dream meets his daughter in a strange house where he eats a raw human heart. We are allowed to turn the screw either way and interpret the story either as a genuine mystical experience, a sacrificial descent to the underworld where the father exchanges his heart for his daughter's life, or else simply as an account of the father's heart attack and his hallucinations under anesthesia.

Mystery and ambiguity are at the heart of Petrushevskaya's fairy tales: we are always inside the dream. Petrushevskaya saves her best clues to the very end, and often we, like the character, have to travel the entire journey without any knowledge of its endpoint and without any memory of the original accident. The final revelation is always somewhat ambiguous, the screw never turns all the way, and the suspense over which reality is more real is never fully broken. When Petrushevskaya finally points the way out of the Orchard of Unusual Possibilities, the question of physical reality has already lost its vital urgency for the reader and the character. The half-memories of abandoned responsibilities, of everyday existence, lose their grip. All that matters now is the enchanting journey itself, and this new unearthly world, and the people you meet there, some of them once loved but long gone and forgotten.

As Solzhenitsyn revealed to the world the insides of the massive prison camps, so Petrushevskaya described for the first time the cramped Soviet apartment on the night of a white wedding, the danger not just of sexual failure but of the mother-in-law barging in drunk. But in all her work—and in the stories in this collection in particular—Petrushevskaya has insisted on a way out. The women in these stories are mad with grief. They walk around with little matchboxes, claiming that a baby is inside ("The Cabbage-patch Mother"); they decide to destroy everything in their apartments and leave in order to thwart an imagined gremlin ("There's Someone in the House"); they appeal to alcoholic homeless prophets for help ("The Miracle"), to their dead mothers ("The Shadow Life"), to the sea god Poseidon. They bury their husbands in the forest, on the street before the draft board, or in the past. They consider burying themselves alongside them—and then they don't. The greatness of Petrushevskaya lies first in her ability to convey the true, crippling power of despair, and then to find a reason to return, as she herself once returned from Lithuania.

She has described the absolute breakdown, in the post-war era, of traditional human values; she has also tried to discover what human relationships can survive. We know of no writer in any language who is working at such a pitch of emotion, with such honesty in even the smallest and shortest stories, with such a profound knowledge of people's dreams and disappointments and consolations.

—KEITH GESSEN AND ANNA SUMMERS

Songs of the Eastern Slavs

The Arm

Dᴜʀɪɴɢ ᴛʜᴇ ᴡᴀʀ, ᴀ ᴄᴏʟᴏɴᴇʟ ʀᴇᴄᴇɪᴠᴇᴅ ᴀ ʟᴇᴛᴛᴇʀ ꜰʀᴏᴍ ʜɪs wife. She misses him very much, it said, and won't he come visit because she's worried she'll die without having seen him. The colonel applied for leave right away, and as it happened that just a few days earlier he'd been awarded a medal, he was granted three days. He got a plane home, but just an hour before his arrival his wife died. He wept, buried his wife, and got on a train back to his base—and then suddenly discovered he had lost his Party card. He dug through all his things, returned to the train station—all this with great difficulty—but couldn't find it. Finally he just went home. There he fell asleep and dreamed that he saw his wife, who said that his Party card was in her coffin—it had fallen out when the colonel bent over to kiss her during the funeral. In his dream his wife also told the colonel not to lift the veil from her face.

The colonel did as he was told: he dug up the coffin, opened it, and found his Party card inside. But then he couldn't resist: he lifted the covering from his wife's face. She lay there as if still alive, but there was a little worm on her left cheek. The colonel wiped away the worm with his hand, covered up his wife's face, and reburied the coffin.

Now he had very little time, and he went directly to the airfield. The plane he needed wasn't there, but then a pilot in a charred jacket pulled him aside and said he was flying to the same place as the colonel and could drop him off. The colonel was surprised that the pilot knew where he was going, but then he saw it was the same pilot who had flown him home.

"Are you all right?" asked the colonel.

"I had a little crash on the way back," said the pilot, "but it's all right. I'll drop you off, it's on the way."

They flew at night. The colonel sat on a metal bench running the length of the plane. In truth he was surprised the plane could fly at all. It was in terrible shape: clumps of material hung everywhere, some kind of charred stump kept rolling into the colonel's feet, and there was a strong odor of burned flesh. They soon landed, and the colonel asked the pilot if he was sure this was the right place. The pilot said he was absolutely sure.

"Why is your plane in such poor shape?" the colonel demanded, and the pilot explained that his navigator usually cleaned up, but he'd just been killed. And right away he started lugging the charred stump off the plane, saying, "There he is, my navigator."

The plane stood in a field, and all through this field wandered wounded men. There was forest in every direction, a campfire burned in the distance, and among the burned-out cars and artillery, people were lying and sitting, others were standing, and others were milling about.

"Damn it!" the colonel yelled. "Where have you brought me? This isn't my base!"

"This is your base now," said the pilot. "I've brought you back to where I picked you up."

The colonel understood that his division had been surrounded and destroyed, everyone killed or wounded, and he cursed everything on earth, including the pilot, who was still messing with his charred stump, which he insisted on calling his navigator, and pleading with it to get up and go.

"Let's start evacuating everyone," ordered the colonel. "We'll begin with the military files, then the coats of arms and the heavily wounded."

"This plane won't fly anymore," the pilot noted.

The colonel drew his pistol and promised to shoot the pilot then and there for disobeying an order. But the pilot ignored him and went on trying to stand the stump on the ground, first one way, then another, saying over and over, "Come on, let's go."

The colonel fired his pistol, but he must have missed because the pilot kept mumbling, "Come on, come on," to his navigator, and in the meantime the roar of vehicles could be heard, and suddenly the field was filled with a mechanized column of German infantry.

The colonel took cover in the grass as the trucks kept coming and coming, but there was neither shooting nor shouting of orders, nor did the motors stop running. Ten minutes later the column was gone, and the colonel raised his head—the pilot was still fussing with his charred stump, and over by the fire people were still lying down, sitting, walking around. The colonel stood and approached the fire. He didn't recognize anyone—this wasn't his division at all. There was infantry here, and artillery, and God knows what else, all in torn uniforms, with open wounds on their arms, legs, stomachs. Only their faces were clean. They talked quietly among themselves. Next to the fire, her back to the colonel, sat a woman in civilian dress with a kerchief on her head.

"Who's the senior officer here?" demanded the colonel. "I need an immediate report on the situation."

No one moved, and no one paid any attention to the colonel when he started shooting, although when the pilot finally managed to roll his charred stump over to them, everyone helped him throw his navigator on the flames and thereby put out the fire. It became completely dark.

The colonel was shivering from the cold and began cursing again: now it would be impossible to get warm, he said— you can't light a fire with a log like that.

And without turning around, the woman by the fire said: "Oh why did you look at my face, why did you lift my veil? Now your arm is going to wither."

It was the voice of the colonel's wife.

The colonel lost consciousness, and when next he woke up he was in a hospital. He was told that they'd found him in the cemetery, next to his wife's grave, and that the arm on which he'd been lying was seriously injured, and now might have to be removed.

Revenge

THERE ONCE LIVED A WOMAN WHO HATED HER NEIGHBOR—A single mother with a small child. As the child grew and learned to crawl, the woman would sometimes leave a pot of boiling water in the corridor, or a container full of bleach, or she'd just spread out a whole box of needles right there in the hall. The poor mother didn't suspect anything—her little girl hadn't learned to walk yet, and she didn't let her out in the corridor during the winter when the floor was cold. But the time was fast approaching when her daughter would be able to leave the room on her own. The mother would say to her neighbor, "Raya, sweetie, you dropped your needles again," at which point Raya would blame her poor memory. "I'm always forgetting things," she'd say.

They'd once been friends. Two unmarried women living in a communal apartment, they had a lot in common. They even shared friends who came by, and on their birthdays they gave each other gifts. They told each other everything. But then Zina became pregnant, and Raya found herself consumed with hatred. She couldn't bear to be in the same apartment as the pregnant woman and began to come home late at night. She couldn't sleep because she kept hearing a man's voice coming from Zina's room; she imagined she heard them talking and moving about, when in fact Zina was living there all by herself.

Zina, on the other hand, grew more and more attached to Raya. She even told her once how wonderful it was to have a neighbor like her, practically an older sister, who would never abandon her in a time of need.

And Raya did in fact help her friend sew clothes in anticipation of the newborn, and she drove Zina to the hospital when the time came. But she didn't come to pick her up after the birth, so that Zina had to stay in the hospital an extra day and ended up taking the baby home wrapped in a ragged hospital blanket that she promised to return right away. Raya explained that she hadn't been feeling well. In the weeks that followed she didn't once go to the store for Zina, or help her bathe the baby, but just sat in her room with warm compresses over her shoulders. She wouldn't even look at the baby, though Zina often took the girl to the bath or the kitchen or just out for a little walk, and kept the door to her room open all the time, as if to say: Come look.

Before the baby came, Zina learned how to use the sewing machine and began to work from home. She had no family to help her, and as for her once-kind neighbor, well, deep down Zina knew she couldn't count on anyone but herself—it had been her idea to have a child, and now she had to bear the burden. When the girl was very little, Zina could take finished clothes to the shop while the baby slept, but when the baby got a little bigger and slept less, Zina's problems began: she had to take the girl with her. Raya continued to complain about her bad joints, and even took time off from work, but Zina wouldn't dare ask her to babysit.

━━┼━━

Meanwhile, Raya was planning the girl's murder. More and more often, as Zina carried the child through the apartment, she would notice a canister on the kitchen floor filled with what was supposed to look like water, or a steaming kettle left precariously balanced on a stool—but still she didn't suspect anything. She continued to play with her daughter just as happily as before, chirping to her, "Say *Mommy*. Say *Mommy*." It's true, though, that when leaving for the store or to drop off her work, Zina began locking the door to her room.

This infuriated Raya. One time when Zina left, the girl woke up and fell out of her crib—at least that's what it sounded like to Raya, who heard something crash to the floor in Zina's room, and then the girl started crying. Raya knew the girl didn't yet walk well on her own, and she must have been badly hurt because she was emitting terrible cries on the other side of the door. Raya couldn't bear them anymore, and finally she put on rubber gloves, poured bleach into a bucket, and began mopping the floors with it, making sure to splash as much as possible under the girl's door. The cries turned into heart-wrenching screams. Raya finished mopping, then washed everything— the bucket, the mop, the gloves—got dressed, and went to a doctor's appointment. After the doctor's, she went to a movie, walked around to some stores, and came home late.

It was dark and quiet behind the door to Zina's room. Raya watched a little bit of television and went to bed. But she couldn't sleep. Zina was gone all night and the whole of the next day. Raya couldn't stand it anymore. She took an ax, broke down the door, and found the room covered with a thin film of dust, with dried spots of blood next to the crib, and a widening trail of blood to the door. There was no trace of the bleach. Raya washed her neighbor's floor, cleaned the room, and sat down to wait, feeling great anticipation.

Finally, after a week, Zina came back home. She said she'd buried her girl and found work on a night shift. That was all she said. Her dark and sunken eyes and her sallow, haggard skin spoke for themselves.

Raya made no attempt to console her neighbor, and life in the apartment came to a standstill. Raya watched television alone while Zina went to work nights and then slept during the day. She seemed to have gone mad from grief and hung photos of her little daughter everywhere. The inflammation in Raya's joints grew worse. She couldn't raise her arms or even walk, and the shots the doctors gave her no longer helped. In the end, Raya couldn't even make herself dinner or put water on to boil. When Zina was home she'd feed Raya herself, but she was home less and less, explaining that it was too painful for her to be there, where her daughter had died. Raya could no longer sleep because of the pain in her shoulders. When she learned that Zina was working at a hospital, she asked her for a strong painkiller, morphine if possible. Zina said she couldn't do it. "I don't smuggle drugs," she said.

"Then I need to take more of these pills," Raya said. "Give me thirty."

"No. I'm not helping you die."

"But I can't do it myself," Raya pleaded.

"You won't get off so easily," Zina said.

So with a superhuman effort, the sick woman lifted the bottle of pills with her mouth, removed the cap, and spilled its entire contents down her throat. Zina sat by the bed. Raya took her time dying. When the sun came up, Zina finally said: "Now you listen to me. I lied to you. My little girl is alive and well. She lives at a preschool, and I work there as a cleaning lady. The stuff you spilled under the door wasn't bleach—it was baking soda. I switched the cans. The blood on the floor was from Lena bumping her nose when she fell out of bed. So it's not your fault. Nothing is your fault.

"But neither is anything my fault. We're even."

And here, on the face of the dying woman, she saw a smile slowly dawn.

Incident at Sokolniki

EARLY IN THE WAR IN MOSCOW THERE LIVED A WOMAN named Lida. Her husband was a pilot, and she didn't love him very much, but they got along well enough. When the war began he was assigned to a base near Moscow, and Lida would visit him there. One time she arrived and was told that his plane had been shot down not far from the airfield, and that the funeral was the next day.

Lida attended the funeral, where she saw three closed coffins, and then returned to her room to find a draft notice for a brigade digging antitank ditches outside the city, and off she went to dig. It was autumn before she finally returned, and she began to notice that she was being followed by a strange young man, very malnourished and pale. Lida would see him on the street and in the store where she bought potatoes with her ration card. One night her doorbell rang and there he was. "Lida, don't you recognize me?" said the man. "I'm your husband." He hadn't been buried at all, it turned out. They had buried some dirt instead of him, whereas his fall from the plane had been broken by the trees in the forest at Sokolniki, and after he'd disentangled himself, he decided not to go back to fighting.

Lida didn't ask how he'd survived these past two and a half months alone in the woods—he told her he found some civilian clothes in an abandoned building—and they began living together again. Lida was nervous the neighbors might notice, but almost everyone had already been evacuated out of Moscow, and so no one did.

Then one day her husband told her that winter was coming soon and they should go right away and bury the flight suit he'd left in the forest.

Lida borrowed a small shovel from the superintendent, and off they went to the forest. They had to take a tram to the Sokolniki station, then follow a brook deep into the woods. No one stopped them, and finally toward evening they reached a wide clearing, and at the edge of it a large pit. It was growing dark. Lida's husband told her that he was too weak to help but that it was important they cover up the pit, since he remembered now that he'd thrown his suit down there.

Lida looked into the pit and saw that, yes, something resembling a flight suit lay at the bottom. She began throwing dirt on top of it, while her husband kept hurrying her along, saying it was getting dark. She shoveled dirt into the pit for three hours, and then, looking up, saw that her husband was gone.

Lida was frightened. She searched for him, running around, then almost fell into the pit and saw that, at the bottom, the flight suit was moving. It was completely dark now, yet somehow Lida made it out of the forest, emerging at her tram stop as the sun was coming up. She rode home, and once she finally got there she fell asleep.

And in her dream her husband came to her and said, "Thank you, Lida, for burying me."

A Mother's Farewell

THERE ONCE LIVED A YOUNG MAN NAMED OLEG WHO WAS left an orphan when his mother died. All he had left was his older sister, for though his father was still alive, that man turned out not to be his real father. Oleg's real father, as he learned when he was going through his mother's papers after her funeral so he could know her better, was some man his mother had met when she was married. In the papers he found a letter from this man saying he already had a family and had no right to abandon his two children for the sake of some future child he wasn't even sure was his. The letter had a date on it. Shortly before Oleg was born, in other words, his mother tried to leave her husband and marry this other man, meaning that things really were as Oleg's sister had once hinted, cruelly and vengefully, in the middle of an argument.

Oleg kept going through the papers and soon found a black folder filled with photographs of his mother in various stages of undress, including completely nude. They were staged photos, as if his mother was performing, and even when nude she wore a long scarf. All of this came as a great blow to Oleg. He'd heard from relatives that as a young woman his mother had been known for her beauty, but the photographs showed a woman already in her mid-thirties, in good shape but not very pretty, merely well-preserved.

After this Oleg, who was sixteen, dropped out of school, dropped out of everything, and for two years, until the day he went off to the army, did nothing, listened to no one, ate what was in the refrigerator, left whenever his father and sister came home, and returned when they were asleep. In the end he collapsed mentally and physically, and his father used his influence to set up an appointment with a medical commission that would declare the boy a schizophrenic and put him on government subsidies and, most important, keep him out of the army. But just before Oleg was to appear before the commission, his father died in his sleep, and everything fell apart. Oleg's sister quickly traded her share of the apartment for an apartment of her own, and left Oleg in his room by himself.

Soon he was drafted.

In the army, Oleg was involved in an incident. He had been placed as a lookout on a mountain path that an escaped prisoner was supposed to be crossing. This man had been on the loose for a month and had already managed to kill five people, including a young woman, and was now about to travel over the only part of the mountain that led away from the prison zone and into the European part of Russia. He wasn't supposed to pass this way for some time, but the ambush was set up in advance, three days in advance, because who knew what kind of transport the prisoner might get his hands on, and maybe he'd get there faster? The ambush consisted of Oleg, a sergeant, and three other soldiers. They sat on a large rock, their machine guns beside them, and took turns at the watch.

It was during Oleg's watch that a man appeared on the trail. He looked like the man whose photograph they'd been shown. Oleg shot him, but it turned out to be the wrong man. He had also been a prisoner once but had served his time and was now going back—although, it's true, he didn't have a permit to move around from place to place. As for the wanted man, he was soon caught on a nearby trail.

Oleg was treated well by the army. They declared him temporarily insane, placed him in a hospital, then discharged him altogether as unfit to serve—and this turned out to be a good deal, since the wife of the man he'd shot kept trying to find the soldier who'd killed her husband when all he'd done was attempt to leave the area without a permit, the poor wretch.

✝

Oleg returned home. He was almost completely bald now, his teeth had fallen out one after the other, he had nothing to eat, nothing to do, and no education to help him find a job. But then out of nowhere his sister appeared, took everything under her control, got Oleg into a vocational program, cleaned up his room, and provided him with groceries and money, even though she wasn't his real sister and had never betrayed any affection for him before.

One night as she was getting ready to go she said off-handedly to Oleg: "You shouldn't believe what I said that time about our mother, you know. Our father was a very suspicious man, that was all. He was a very difficult person and could have driven anyone insane."

Then she left.

As soon as she was gone Oleg took out the suitcase with his mother's papers. This time all he found was an envelope with photos of her funeral. The folder where the nude photos had been now contained a single sheet of crumpled old black paper, which dissolved into dust as soon as he tried to touch it.

Oleg began rifling through the papers. Everywhere he looked were letters from his mother to his father, the father he'd grown up with, speaking of love, of faithfulness, of Oleg's resemblance to him. Oleg cried all night, and the next morning he got up to wait for his sister to tell her how he'd lost his mind when he was sixteen, and imagined some terrible things, and even killed a man because of it—for the man he'd shot didn't look at all like the photograph of the real criminal.

But his sister never came. She must have forgotten about him, and that was all right because he soon forgot about her, too—he was busy with his new life. He finished the vocational program, went to college, got married, had children.

And what was funny was that both he and his wife had dark eyes and dark hair, but their two sons were blue-eyed and blond, just like their grandmother, Oleg's dead mother.

One time his wife suggested they visit his mother's grave. It took a long time to find it: the cemetery was old and the gravestones crowded together, and also, on his mother's grave, right in the middle, there stood another, smaller headstone.

"That must be my father," said Oleg, who had not attended his father's funeral.

"No, look," said his wife, "it's your sister."

Oleg was horrified—how could he have neglected his sister like this?—and he bent down to read the inscription. It really was his sister.

"Except the dates are wrong," he said. "My sister came to visit me much later than that, after I came home from the army. Remember I told you how she got me back on my feet? She literally saved my life. I was young, and small things were always sending me over the edge."

"That can't be," his wife said. "They never get the dates wrong. When did you come back from the army?"

And they began to argue, standing there at the foot of his mother's unkempt grave. The wild grass, which had grown considerably over the summer months, reached to their knees until, at long last, they bent down and started clearing it.

Allegories

Hygiene

ONE TIME THE DOORBELL RANG AT THE APARTMENT OF the R. family, and the little girl ran to answer it. A young man stood before her. In the hallway light he appeared to be ill, with extremely delicate, pink, shiny skin. He said he'd come to warn the family of an immediate danger: There was an epidemic in the town, an illness that killed in three days. People turned red, they swelled up, and then, mostly, they died. The chief symptom was the appearance of blisters, or bumps. There was some hope of surviving if you observed strict personal hygiene, stayed inside the apartment, and made sure there were no mice around—since mice, as always, were the main carriers of the disease.

The girl's grandparents listened to the young man, as did her father and the girl herself. Her mother was in the bath.

"I survived the disease," the young man said simply, and removed his hat to reveal a bald scalp covered with the thinnest layer of pink skin, like the foam atop boiling milk. "I survived," he went on, "and because of this I'm now immune. I'm going door to door to deliver bread and other supplies to people who need them. Do you need anything? If you give me the money, I'll go to the store—and a bag, too, if you have one. Or a shopping cart. There are long lines now in front of the stores, but I'm immune to the disease."

"Thank you," said the grandfather, "but we're fine."

"If your family gets sick, please leave your doors open. I've picked out four buildings—that's all I can handle. If any of you should survive, as I did, you can help me rescue others, and lower corpses out."

"What do you mean, lower corpses out?" asked the grandfather.

"I've worked out a system for evacuating the bodies. We'll throw them out into the street. But we'll need large plastic bags; I don't know where to get those. The factories make double-layered plastic sheets, which we could use, although I don't have the money. You could cut those sheets with a hot knife, and the material will seal back together automatically to form a bag. All you really need is a hot knife and double-layered plastic."

"Thank you, but we're fine," repeated the grandfather.

So the young man went along the hall to the other apartments like a beggar, asking for money. As the R. family closed the door behind him, he was already ringing their neighbors' bell. The door opened a little, on its chain, leaving just a crack, so the young man was forced to lift his hat and tell his story to the crack. The R. family heard the neighbor reply abruptly, but apparently the young man didn't leave, for there were no footsteps. Another door opened slightly: someone else wanted to hear his story. Finally a laughing voice said: "If you have some money already, run and get me ten bottles of vodka. I'll pay you back."

They heard footsteps, and then it was quiet.

"When he comes back," said the grandmother, "he should bring us some bread and condensed milk, and some eggs. And soon we'll need more cabbage and potatoes."

"He's a charlatan," said the grandfather. "But those aren't burns; they look like something else."

Finally the father snapped to attention and led the girl away from the door. These were his wife's parents, not his, and he rarely agreed with them about anything. Nor did they exactly ask his opinion. Something really was happening, he felt: it couldn't help but happen. He'd been sensing it for a long time now, and waiting. For the moment he was experiencing a temporary stupor. He walked the little girl out of the foyer— there was no need for her to stand there until the mysterious stranger knocked again. The father needed to have a serious talk with the stranger, man to man, about treatment options, escape routes, and the overall circumstances on the ground.

The grandparents stayed at the door, because they could hear that the elevator hadn't been called up. The young man would still be on their floor. He was probably asking for all the money and shopping bags at once so that he wouldn't have to run back and forth. Or else he really was a charlatan and a crook and was collecting the money only for himself, something the grandmother knew a little about since the time a woman knocked at their door and said she lived in the next entryway and that an old lady, Baba Nura, had died there. She was sixty-nine. The woman was collecting money for the funeral, and she held out a list of people who'd donated, their signatures, and the sums they'd given: thirty kopeks, a ruble, even two rubles. The grandmother gave the woman a ruble, though she couldn't actually recall anyone named Nura—and no wonder, because five minutes later one of their nice neighbors rang the doorbell and said that they should be careful, some woman no one knew, a crook, was soliciting money under false pretenses. She had two men waiting on the second floor, and they took off with the money, dropping the list of names and sums to the floor.

The grandparents were still at the door, listening. Nikolai joined them; he didn't want to miss anything. His wife, Elena, came out of the shower at last and started asking loudly what was going on, but they hushed her up.

Yet they heard no more doorbells. The elevator kept going up and down, and people got out on the sixth floor and made noise with their keys and their door slamming. This meant it could not have been the young man: he didn't have any keys. He'd have had to ring the doorbell.

Finally Nikolai turned on the television, and they had supper. Nikolai ate a great deal. He ate so much the grandfather felt compelled to make a remark. Elena came to her husband's defense, and then the little girl asked why everyone was arguing, and family life went on its way.

⸸

That night, on the street, someone shattered what sounded like a very large window.

"It's the bakery," said the grandfather, looking down from the balcony. "Run, Kolya, get us some supplies."

They began to collect equipment for Nikolai to go out. A police car drove up, arrested someone, and drove off, leaving a police officer posted at the bakery door. Nikolai went downstairs with a backpack and a knife. By then a whole crowd had gathered outside. They surrounded the policeman, knocked him down, and then people began jumping in and out of the bakery. A woman was mugged for a suitcase filled with bread. They put a hand over her mouth and dragged her away. The crowd kept growing.

Nikolai returned with a very full backpack—thirty kilos of pretzels and ten loaves of bread. Still standing on the landing, he removed all his clothes and threw them down the trash chute. He soaked cotton balls in eau-de-cologne, wiped down his body, and threw them down the chute as well. The grandfather, very pleased with the new developments, restricted himself to just one remark—the R. family would have to budget their eau-de-cologne.

In the morning, Nikolai ate a kilo of pretzels all by himself. The grandfather wore dentures and dipped the hard pretzels lugubriously into his tea. The grandmother seemed depressed and didn't say anything, while Elena tried to force her little daughter to eat more pretzels. Finally the grandmother broke down and insisted that they ration the food. They couldn't go out robbing every night, she said, and look, the bakery was all boarded up—everything had already been taken away!

So the R. family's supplies were counted up and divided. During lunch Elena gave her portion to her daughter. Nikolai was as gloomy as a thundercloud, and after lunch he ate a whole loaf of black bread by himself.

They had supplies enough for a week.

Nikolai and Elena both called into work, but no one answered. They called some friends: everyone was sitting home, waiting. The television stopped working, its screen blank and flickering. The next day the phone stopped working. Out on the street, people walked along with shopping bags and backpacks. Someone had sawed down a young tree and was dragging it home through the empty yard.

It was time to figure out what to do with the cat, which hadn't eaten in two days and was meowing terribly on the balcony.

"We need to let her in and feed her," said the grandfather. "Cats are a valuable source of fresh, vitamin-rich meat."

Nikolai let the cat in, and they fed it some soup—not very much, no need to overfeed it after its fast. The little girl wouldn't leave the cat's side; while it had been on the balcony, the girl kept throwing herself at the balcony door to try and touch her. Now she could feed the little creature to her heart's content, though eventually even her mother couldn't take it. "You're feeding her what I tear out of my mouth to give to you!" she cried. There were now enough supplies for five days.

Everyone waited for something to happen, some sort of mobilization to be announced. On the third night they heard the roar of motors outside. It was the army leaving town.

"They'll reach the outskirts and set up a quarantine," said the grandfather. "No one gets in, no one gets out. The scariest part is that it all turned out to be true, what the young man said. We'll have to go into town for food."

"If you give me your cologne, I'll go," said Nikolai. "I'm almost out."

"Everything will be yours soon enough," the grandfather said meaningfully. He'd lost a lot of weight. "It's a miracle the plumbing still works."

"Don't jinx it!" snapped his wife.

Nikolai left that night for the store. He took the shopping bags and the backpack, as well as a knife and a flashlight. He came back while it was still dark, undressed on the stairs, threw the clothes into the trash chute, and, naked, wiped himself down with the cologne. Wiping one foot, he stepped into the apartment; only then did he wipe the other foot. He crushed the cotton balls together and threw them out the door, then dipped the backpack in a pot of boiling water, and also the canvas shopping bags. He hadn't gotten much: soap, matches, salt, some oatmeal, jelly, and decaffeinated coffee. The grandfather was extremely pleased, however—he was positively beaming. Nikolai held the knife over a burner on the stove.

"Blood," the grandfather noted approvingly before going to bed, "that's the most infectious thing of all."

They had enough food now for ten days, according to their calculations, if they subsisted on jelly and oatmeal, and all ate very little.

Nikolai started going out every night, and now there was the question of his clothing. He would fold it into a cellophane bag while he was still on the stairs, and each time he came in he would disinfect the knife over a burner. He still ate plenty, though without any remarks, now, from his father-in-law.

The cat grew skinnier by the hour. Her fur was hanging loose on her, and meals were torturous, for the girl kept trying to throw bits of food onto the floor for the cat as Elena rapped the girl on the knuckles. They were all yelling, now, all the time. They'd throw the cat out of the kitchen and close the door, and then the cat would begin hurling itself against the door to get back in.

Eventually this led to a horrifying scene. The grandparents were sitting in the kitchen when the girl appeared with the cat in her arms. Both their mouths were smeared with something.

"That's my girl," said the girl to the cat—and kissed it, probably not for the first time, on its filthy mouth.

"What are you doing?" the grandmother cried.

"She caught a mouse," said the girl. "She ate it." And once again the girl kissed the cat on the mouth.

"What mouse?" asked the grandfather. He and his wife sat still with shock.

"A gray one."

"A puffy one? A fat one?"

"Yes, it was fat and big," said the girl happily. The cat, in the girl's arms, was trying to free herself.

"Hold her tight!" yelled the grandfather. "Go to your room now, girl, go on. Take the kitty. You've really done it now, haven't you?" His voice was growing louder. "You little tramp! You brat! You've played your games with your kitty, haven't you?"

"Don't yell," said the girl. She ran quickly to her room.

The grandfather followed, spraying her path with cologne. He secured the door behind her with a chair, then called in Nikolai, who was resting after a sleepless night outside. Elena was sleeping with him. They woke up reluctantly; everything was discussed and settled. Elena began crying and tearing out her hair. From the child's room they could hear knocking.

"Let me out, open up, I need to go to the bathroom!"

"Listen to me!" yelled Nikolai. "Stop yelling!"

"You're yelling!" cried the girl. "Let me out, please let me out!"

Nikolai and the others went into the kitchen. They were forced to keep Elena in the bathroom. She was beating on her door, too.

By evening the girl had calmed down. Nikolai asked her if she'd managed to pee. With difficulty the girl answered that, yes, she'd gone in her underwear. She asked for something to drink.

There was a child-sized bed in the girl's room, a rug, a locked wardrobe with all the family's clothing, and some bookshelves. It had been a cozy room for a little girl; now it was a quarantine chamber. Nikolai managed to hack an opening high up in the door. He lowered a bottle filled with soup and bread crumbs through the hole. The girl was told to eat this for dinner and then to urinate in the bottle and pour it out the window. But the window was locked at the top, and the girl couldn't reach, and the bottle turned out to be too narrow for her to aim into. Excrement should have been easy enough: she was to take a few pages from one of the books and go on those, and then throw this all out the window. Nikolai had fashioned a slingshot and after three attempts had managed to put a fairly large hole in the window.

But the girl soon showed the signs of her spoiled upbringing. She was unable to defecate onto the pages as she was supposed to. She couldn't keep track of her own needs. Elena would ask her twenty times a day whether she needed to go poo; the girl would say no, she didn't; and five minutes later she'd soil herself.

Meanwhile, the girl's food situation was becoming impossible: There were a finite number of bottles, and the girl was unable to retie the ones she had used to the rope. There were already nine bottles scattered on the floor when the girl stopped coming to the door or answering questions. The cat must have been sitting on her, though it hadn't appeared in their line of vision in a while, ever since Nikolai started trying to shoot it with the slingshot. The girl had been feeding the cat half of every ration—she'd simply pour it out on the floor for her. Now the girl no longer answered questions, and her little bed stood by the wall, outside their line of vision.

They'd spent three days innovating, struggling to arrange things for the girl, attempting to teach her how to wipe herself (until now Elena had done this for her), getting water to her so she could somehow wash herself—and pleading interminably for her to come to the door to receive her bottle of food. One time Nikolai decided to wash the girl by pouring a bucket of hot water on her, instead of lowering the food, and after that the girl was afraid to come to the door. All this had so exhausted the inhabitants of the apartment that when the girl finally stopped answering them, they all lay down and slept for a long, long time.

Then everything ended very quickly. Waking up, the grand-parents discovered the cat in their bed with that same bloody mouth—apparently the cat had started eating the girl, but had climbed out the makeshift window, possibly to get a drink. Nikolai appeared in the doorway, and after hearing what had happened slammed the door shut and began to move things around on the other side, locking them in with a chair. The door remained closed. Nikolai did not want to cut an opening; he put this off. Elena yelled and screamed and tried to remove the chair, but Nikolai once again locked her in the bathroom.

Then Nikolai lay down on the bed for a moment, and began to swell up, until his skin had distended horribly. The night before, he'd killed a woman for her backpack, and then, right on the street, he'd eaten a can of buckwheat concentrate. He just wanted to try it, but ended up eating the whole thing, he couldn't help himself. Now he was sick.

Nikolai figured out quickly that he was sick, but it was too late—he was already swelling up. The entire apartment shook with all the knocks on all the doors. The cat was crying, and the apartment above them had also reached the knocking phase, but Nikolai just kept pushing, as if in labor, until finally the blood started coming out of his eyes, and he died, not thinking of anything, just pushing and hoping to get free of it soon.

And no one opened the door onto the landing, which was too bad, because the young man was making his rounds, carrying bread with him. All the knocking in the apartment of the R. family had died down, with only Elena still scratching at her door a little, not seeing anything, as blood came out of her eyes. What was there to see, anyway, in a dark bathroom, while lying on the floor?

Why was the young man so late? He had many apartments under his care, spread across four enormous buildings. He reached their entryway for the second time only on the night of the sixth day—three days after the girl had stopped answering, one full day after Nikolai succumbed, twenty hours after Elena's parents passed away, and five minutes after Elena herself.

But the cat kept meowing, like in that famous story where the man kills his wife and buries her behind a brick wall in his basement, and when the police come they hear the meowing behind the wall and figure out what happened, because along with the wife's body the husband has entombed her favorite cat, which has stayed alive by eating her flesh.

The cat meowed and meowed, and the young man, hearing this lone living sound in the entire entryway, where all the knocking and screaming had by now gone silent, decided to fight at least for this one life. He found a metal rod lying in the yard, covered in blood, and with it he broke down the door.

What did he see there? A familiar black mound in the bathroom, a black mound in the living room, two black mounds behind a door held shut with a chair. That's where the cat slipped out. It nimbly jumped through a primitive makeshift window in another door, and behind that door the young man heard a human voice. He removed a chair blocking the way and entered a room filled with broken glass, rubbish, excrement, pages torn out of books, strewn bottles, and headless mice. A little girl with a bright-red bald scalp, just like the young man's, only redder, lay on the bed. She stared at the young man, and the cat sat beside her on her pillow, also staring attentively at him, with big, round eyes.

A New Soul

YOU CAN RECOGNIZE THEM, BUT ONLY IF YOU YOURSELF ARE one of them. There are signs, and each sign happens twice. Those who see the signs don't ever understand what they're seeing. The heart flutters for a second, that's all. A tear clouds the eye, but the memory remains out of reach. Twin souls have passed one another in space.

It's also called love at first sight (and you may never have that sight again).

The double sign, the light from the proper direction, a house lit up by it—then the person will recognize the place. But everything that came before, and after, and why this place, and why this light, this house, this wind—the exiled soul won't ever understand it. The soul will never return to that former time, that other life. It needs to drag along in this current one, unfortunately.

Because it's the former life that's always dearest to us. *That*'s the life colored by sadness, by love—that's where we left everything connected to what we call our feelings. Now everything is different; life just carries on, without joy, without tears.

But this is all a prologue. The fact is a man is rushing home from a business trip. He's late for his flight, he's caught a cab, they raced to the airport, but the cab got pulled over, the driver had to pay a fine, that took up precious minutes, and arriving finally at the gate the man finds nothing: the plane is gone.

He was rushing, this man, because the next morning his son is being drafted into the army—suddenly, without any warning, they're taking him right out of college. The man learned about it this evening: he'd finally gotten a chance to call home from the post office to say that everything was fine, he was catching a flight in the morning, to which his wife barked back—"It'll be too late!"—before telling him the news. So off he went—to say good-bye! Their beloved, only child was leaving for two years; their clumsy little boy, unprepared for the difficulties, and cruelties, for the ways of the army—their gentle little boy, loving, domestic, kind. He was always getting beaten up in the yard when he was little; in school there'd also been problems and sadists; now he was at the university, all that was behind them. He'd found friends like himself, well-mannered, thoughtful boys and girls—and suddenly there you go, they're taking him in the morning.

This man, the father, was no longer young, and the mother also was no longer very young. They'd met when neither of them was very young, and gave birth, miraculously, to this joy, this angel, whose peers, the parents believed, didn't appreciate him, as a tribe never appreciates its first prophet.

The father already had a daughter—his elderly daughter, as he liked to say, which was true, actually. She was the product of an early marriage, and what's more the girl's mother was older than the father by eleven years. Their marriage collapsed when he was forty-two and she fifty-three—how do you like that? A desperate age for husband and wife both. And then suddenly the husband met the love of his life. She too was not young, but was full of tenderness, with a cloud of hair around her golden head and blue eyes—she had just joined his firm. Everything was settled for them, and then they gave birth to this miracle, a fragile, golden-haired angel of a son. They lived together for eighteen years and a smidgeon, clinging to each other, living what seemed like an extra, bonus life, but always worrying about their little boy.

And finally the payment had come due—the tears and threats of the first wife, her curse had come to pass: may everything that you put me through return to you in spades.

The father has missed the plane. Nor are there any seats on the morning flight.

He gets a partial refund for his plane ticket and hurls himself into the late bus, which takes him to the train station, where he somehow manages, tearfully, to say something to the conductor, a few simple words about his son, so that she steps aside and allows him on the train—which is already moving—and even, after hearing his few simple words, puts him into her own compartment, which is overheated, and where, on the top bunk, the father lies in torment until the morning. As soon as the train arrives he races to the apartment, but it is already empty: things are scattered on the floor; the phone is off the hook, beeping; his son's unmade bed gapes like the bed of a condemned man on the day of his execution.

The father quickly finds his bearings, learns the address of the draft board from a neighbor in the next entryway, where his son's classmate lives—the boy was in fact his son's tormentor, but who cares about that now. That boy's grandmother tells the father where to run; her own family has gone to see off their child after a night of partying.

The father makes it in time. He sees his son a crowd of pale, hungover, moronic, defeated boys.

The father takes hold of his son's sleeve, begins to scream, and wakes up in the United States, in the form of an unhappy immigrant named Grisha, who's been abandoned by his hardworking wife six months after they arrived in the States. She went to work as a cleaning lady at the mall and then married a professor, an old childhood friend, whom she'd accidentally met there. A happy coincidence! And she cast Grisha away like an old rag.

At the moment we're describing, Grisha has just been released from the mental hospital, where, not knowing the language, he'd spent all his time in front of the television, though without participating in the vicious arguments about which channel to put on. He'd landed in the mental ward after his third unsuccessful suicide attempt.

Somehow or other, one day he began to talk in an impoverished television language with a crazy black man, who was always yelling—nonstop—about how he was going to kill all the white people, that filth, how he'd killed ten of them already and he wanted to kill an eleventh, he was willing to go to the electric chair for it, to become a martyr for his beliefs. He was the first one Grisha understood, and he answered him in his own way, in the voice of a television anchorman. Kill me, said Grisha. Go ahead, *pleeze*—strangle me, if you'd like, or some other way, I don't care, said Grisha, utterly surprised by his ability to form English words, and unaware that the soul of that unhappy father was already knocking about inside him and that it knew many things (including five languages). The weeping Grisha was taken to his room and tranquilized.

The black man, Jim, was stopped short, knocked from his imaginary universe of righteous racial vengeance by this actual white person who was asking for his own death. Jim began wondering whether he could do it—commit this act for, he claimed to himself, the eleventh time, and immediately he went to find out what had happened to this piece of filth, who had turned out in fact to be a dirty Russian, which on the table of ranks in Jim's head placed him below just about everyone. Jim was, after all, a full-fledged citizen of the United States.

And he began to defend the rights of this dirty Russian. He taught him to recognize the main enemies of democracy on television—the senators and presidents and newspeople who spread their lies. Jim taught Grisha a great many things, nodding his wise old head and spinning his thin fingers, and Grisha just kept crying.

He didn't know he was crying for his wife and son, whom he'd left that day in the Moscow street outside the draft board, weeping on their knees next to his body. He didn't know that the boy hadn't been taken into the army after all, that his wife had managed to hide him even while herself wailing terribly. That is to say she wept loudly next to the body of her collapsed husband but in the meantime whispered to the boy, "Hide out at your Aunt Valya's in the country," and off he'd gone even before the ambulance arrived.

Grisha wandered around, weeping, unable to reach himself. He discovered a little hole below his neck, like an extra eye, from which tears poured out. He saw strange dreams—in which a cloudless joy and love surrounded him, sang lullabies to him, calmed him.

The shots they gave him made him dizzy, high, and caused him to stop crying, but the little eye below his neck kept pouring out tears.

With time the shock subsided, and Grisha was released while Jim was transferred to another building, where he found himself a protégé in the form of a little black-and-white kitten, from whom he never parted, as it too was a member of an oppressed race—America had no room in its heart for a homeless kitten. But he'd come from somewhere, and Jim had found him, and when visiting Grisha to say good-bye he showed him the little treasure in his hands.

And Grisha eventually returned to his cave. He rented a basement room from a Russian woman—it had a toilet but no bath.

†

Not long after his release from the hospital, Grisha's landlady had a visitor—her cousin, a sad-looking gray-haired widow with a son back in Moscow. Grisha caught just a glimpse of her while going down to his basement; she was sitting on the porch drinking tea. She was stirring and stirring the tea with a spoon, and a speck of reflected light danced upon her face. Her face was tearful, dead.

The woman stirred the spoon in her tea listlessly, and the little point of light bouncing off the surface of the tea blinked on her little red nose and in her blue eye. The blue eye especially was lit up in a very poetic way—it flashed like some living precious jewel.

It was a genuine double recognition: two souls met and didn't know it.

Five minutes later, Grisha was up the stairs and sitting across from this old woman, this widow. His landlady, her cousin, had gone off to the college where she taught. This old woman never did get around to drinking any of her tea or lifting her gaze. Grisha fell in love with her with all his brokeh heart, married her, and came to Moscow to meet her melancholy, pale, blond and curly-haired son.

When he shook hands with this son, this Alyosha, a tear rolled from the third, unseen eye below Grisha's neck—a bitter, tiny tear from the dead father. Alyosha avoided the draft in the end: his father had died, as Grisha's new wife explained it, and so the son became the lone provider for a pensioner (his mother), and by law such a person is exempt from army service. At the draft board that day they kept yelling and insisting that he should start serving now, they'd release him later (they needed to fill a quota, apparently, and without him they'd be one short). So the mother had to run around

and gather the necessary papers while Alyosha was hiding—
the police would come to the apartment at night looking for
him—and meanwhile the funeral had to be arranged! Grisha
listened to all these tales and wept every time, no matter how
often he heard them.

But Alyosha never accepted this new father. He was
shocked by the speed with which his mother had experienced
a change of heart. It seemed like a betrayal—she still wore
the same slippers she wore while his father lived, and now
she'd flung herself into another marriage. Alyosha refused to
go to America with them. But his mother, looking younger
than herself by twenty years, blossoming, golden-haired,
blue-eyed, in love, flew off with her new husband to the place
where her first husband's soul now lived—and no one ever
did explain it to either of them.

The New Robinson Crusoes

A Chronicle of the End of the Twentieth Century

So MY PARENTS DECIDED THEY WOULD OUTSMART EVERYONE.
When it began they piled me and a load of canned food into
a truck and took us to the country, the far-off and forgotten
country, somewhere beyond the Mur River. We'd bought a
cabin there for cheap a few years before, and mostly it just
stood there. We'd go at the end of June to pick wild straw-
berries (for my health), and then once more in August in time
for stray apples and plums and black cranberries in the abandoned orchards, and for raspberries and mushrooms in the
woods. The cabin was falling apart when we bought it, and
we never fixed anything. Then one fine day late in the spring,
after the mud had hardened a little, my father arranged things
with a man with a truck, and off we went with our groceries,
just like the new Robinson Crusoes, with all kinds of yard
tools and a rifle and a bloodhound called Red—who could,
theoretically, hunt rabbits.

Now my father began his feverish activity. Over in the
garden he plowed the earth—plowing the neighbors' earth
in the process, so that he pulled out our fence posts and

planted them in the next yard. We dug up the vegetable patch, planted three sacks of potatoes, groomed the apple trees. My father went into the woods and brought back some turf for the winter. And suddenly too we had a wheelbarrow. In general my father was very active in the storerooms of our neighbors' boarded-up houses, picking up whatever might come in handy: nails, old boards, shingles, pieces of tin, buckets, benches, door handles, windowpanes, and all sorts of useful old things, like well buckets, yarn spinners, grandfather clocks, and then not-so-useful old things, like old iron teakettles, iron oven parts, stove tops, and so on.

Three old women were the village's sole inhabitants: Baba Anisya; Marfutka, who had reverted to semi-savagery; and the red-headed Tanya, the only one with a family: her kids would come around and bring things, and take other things away—which is to say they'd bring canned food from the city, cheese, butter, and cookies, and take away pickled cucumbers, cabbage, potatoes. Tanya had a rich basement pantry and a good, enclosed front yard, and one of her grandchildren, a permanently ailing boy named Valera, often stayed with her. His ears were always hurting, or else he was covered with eczema. Tanya herself was a nurse by training, which training she received in a labor camp in Kolyma, where she'd been sent at the age of seventeen for stealing a suckling pig at her collective farm. She was popular, and she kept her stove warm—the shepherdess Vera would come from the next village over and call out (I could hear her in the distance), "Tanya, put the tea on! Tanya, put the tea on!" Baba Anisya, the only human being in the village—Marfutka didn't count, and Tanya was a criminal—said that Tanya used to be the head of the health clinic here, practically the most important person around. Anisya worked for her for five years, for doing which she lost her pension because it meant she didn't complete the full twenty-five years at the collective farm, and then five years sweeping up at the clinic don't count, especially with a boss like Tanya. My mom made a trip once with Anisya to the regional Party headquarters in Priozersk, but the headquarters had been boarded up long ago, everything was boarded up, and my mother walked the twenty-five kilometers home with a frightened Baba Anisya, who immediately began digging in her garden with renewed vigor, and chopping wood, and carrying firewood and twigs into her house—she was fending off a hungry death, which is what she'd face if she did nothing, like Marfutka, who was eighty-five and no longer lit her stove, and even the few potatoes she'd managed to drag into her house had frozen during the winter. They simply lay there in a wet, rotten pile. Marfutka had nibbled out of that pile all winter and now refused to part with these riches, her only ones, when one time my mother sent me over with a shovel to clean them out. Marfutka refused to open the door, looking out through the window that was draped in rags and seeing that I was carrying a garden spade. Either she ate the potatoes raw, despite her lack of teeth, or she made a fire for them when no one was looking—it was impossible to tell. She had no firewood. In the spring Marfutka, wrapped in layers of greasy shawls, rags, and blankets, showed up at Anisya's warm home and sat there like a mummy, not breathing a word. Anisya didn't even try to talk to her, and Marfutka just sat there. I looked once at her face, which is to say what was visible of her face under the rags, and saw that it was small and dark, and that her eyes were like wet holes.

Marfutka survived another winter but no longer went into the yard—she'd decided, apparently, to die of hunger. Anisya said simply that, last year, Marfutka still had some life left in her, but this year she's done for, her feet don't look straight ahead but at each other, the wrong way. One day my mother took me along, and we planted half a bucket of potatoes in Marfutka's yard, but Marfutka just looked at us and worried, it was clear, that we were taking over her plot, though she didn't have the energy to walk over to us. My mother just went over to her and handed her some potatoes, but Marfutka, thinking her plot was being bought from her for half a bucket of potatoes, grew very frightened, and refused.

That evening we all went over to Anisya's for some goat milk. Marfutka was there. Anisya said she'd seen us on Marfutka's plot. My mother answered that we'd decided to help Baba Marfa. Anisya didn't like it. Marfutka was going to the next world, she said, she didn't need help, she'd find her way. It should be added that we were paying Anisya for the milk in canned food and soup packets. This couldn't go on forever, since the goat made more milk every day, whereas the canned food was dwindling. We needed to establish a more stable equivalent, and so directly after the discussion about Marfutka, my mother said that our canned foods were running out, we didn't have anything to eat ourselves, so we wouldn't be buying any more milk that day. Clever Anisya grasped the point at once and answered that she'd bring us a can of milk the next day and we could talk about it—if we still had potatoes, that is. She was angry, apparently, that we were wasting our potatoes on Marfutka instead of paying her. She didn't know how many potatoes we'd invested in Marfutka's plot during the hungry spring. Her imagination was working like a little engine. She must have been calculating that Marfutka didn't have long to go and that she'd gather her harvest in the fall, and was angry in advance that we were the rightful owners of those planted potatoes. Everything becomes complicated when it's a matter of surviving in times like these, especially for an old, not particularly strong person in the face of a strong young family—my parents were both forty-two then, and I was eighteen.

That night we received a visit from Tanya, who wore a city coat and yellow rubber boots, and carried a new bag in her hands. She brought us a little piglet smothered by its mother, wrapped in a clean rag. Then she wondered if we were officially registered to live in the village. She pointed out that many of the houses here had owners, and that the owners might want to come out and see for themselves what was happening, say if someone were to write them, and that all that we beheld was not just riches lying by the roadside. In conclusion, Tanya reminded us that we'd encroached on the plot of our neighbor, and that Marfutka was still alive. As for the piglet, she offered to sell it to us for money, that is for paper rubles, and that night my father chopped and pickled the little pig, which in the rag looked like a little baby. It had lashes above its eyes and everything.

After Tanya left, Anisya came by with a can of goat's milk, and over tea we quickly negotiated a new price—one can of food for three days of milk. With hatred in her voice Anisya asked why Tanya had come by, and she approved of our decision to help Marfutka, though she said of her with a laugh that she smelled bad.

The milk and the piglet were supposed to protect us from scurvy, and what's more Anisya was raising a little goat, and we'd decided to buy it for ten cans of food—but only a little later, after it had grown some more, since Anisya knew better how to raise a goat. We never discussed this with Anisya, though, and one day she came over, full of insane jealousy at her old boss Tanya, and proudly showed us that she'd killed her little goat and wrapped it up for us. Two cans of fish were the answer she received, and my mom burst into tears. We tried to eat the meat—we broiled it—but it was inedible, and my father ended up pickling it again.

My mom and I did manage to buy a baby goat. We walked ten kilometers to the village of Tarutino, but we did it as if we were tourists, as if it were old times. We wore backpacks, and sang as we walked, and when we got to the village we asked where we could drink some goat's milk, and when we bought a glass of milk from a peasant woman for a bread roll, we made a show of our affection for the little goats. I started whispering to my mother, as if I wanted a goat for myself. The peasant woman became very excited, sensing a customer, but my mother whispered back no, at which point the woman began speaking very sweetly to me, saying she loved the little goats like her own children and because of this she'd give them both to me. To which I quickly replied, "No, I only need one!" We agreed on a price right away; the woman clearly didn't know the state of the ruble and took very little, and even threw in a handful of salt crystals for the road. She obviously thought she'd made a good deal, and, in truth, the little goat did begin to fade away pretty quickly after the long walk home. It was Anisya again who got us out of it. She gave the baby goat to her own big goat, but first she covered it with some mud from her yard, and the goat took it as one of her own, didn't kill it. Anisya beamed with pride.

We now had all the essentials, but my indomitable father, despite his slight limp, started going out into the forest, and every day he went farther and farther. He would take his ax, and some nails, and a saw, and a wheelbarrow—he'd leave with the sunrise and come back with the night. My mother and I waded around the garden, somehow or other kept up my father's work of collecting window panes, doors, and glass, and then of course we made the food, cleaned up, lugged the water for laundry, sewed, and mended. We'd collect old, forgotten sheepskin coats in the abandoned houses and then sew something like fur ponchos for the winter, and also we made mittens and some fur mattresses for the beds. My father, when he noticed such a mattress one night on his bed, immediately rolled up all three and carted them away the next morning. It looked like he was preparing another refuge for us, except this one would be deep in the forest, and later on it came in very handy. But it also turned out that no amount of labor and no amount of foresight can save you, no one and nothing can save you except luck.

In the meantime we lived through the hungriest month, June, which is when the supplies in a village usually run out. We shoved chopped dandelions into our mouths, made soup out of weeds, but for the most part we just gathered grass, pulled handfuls of it, and carried it, carried it, carried it home in sacks. We didn't know how to mow it, and anyway it hadn't really risen high enough for mowing yet. Finally Anisya gave us a scythe (in exchange for ten sackfuls of grass, which is not nothing), and Mom and I took turns mowing. I should repeat: We were far from the world, I missed my friends and girlfriends, and nothing reached us anymore. My father turned on the radio sometimes, but only rarely, because he wanted to conserve the batteries. The radio was full of lies and falsehoods anyway, and we just mowed and mowed, and our little goat Raya was growing and we needed to find her a boy goat. We trod over to the next village again, but the peasant woman was unfriendly to us now—by this point everyone knew all about us, but they didn't know we had a goat, since Anisya was raising it, so the woman thought we'd lost Raya, and to hell with us. She wouldn't give us the other goat, and we didn't have any bread now—there wasn't any flour, so there wasn't any bread—and anyway her little goat had grown, too, and she knew three kilos of fresh meat would mean a lot of money in this hungry time. We finally got her to agree to sell the goat for a kilo of salt and ten bars of soap. But for us this meant future milk, and we ran home to get our payment, telling the woman we wanted the goat alive. "Don't worry," she answered, "I'm not bloodying my hands for you." That evening we brought the little goat home, and then began the tough summer days: mowing the grass, weeding the plot, grooming the potato plants, and all of this at the same pace as experienced Anisya—we'd arranged with her that we'd take half the goats' manure, and somehow or other we fertilized the plot, but our vegetables still grew poorly and mostly produced weeds. Baba Anisya, freed from mowing grass, would tie up the big goat and its little kindergarten in a place where we could see them, and then scramble off into the woods for mushrooms and berries, after which she'd come by our plot and examine the fruits of our labor. We had to replant the dill, which we'd planted too deeply; we needed it for pickling cucumbers. The potatoes flourished mostly above ground level. My mother and I read *The Guide to Planting and Sowing,* and my father finally finished his work in the forest, and we went to look at his new home. It turned out to be someone's hut, which my father had refurbished by putting in window frames, glass, and doors, and covering the roof with tar. The house was empty. From then on at night we carried tables and benches and crates and buckets and iron pots and pans and our remaining supplies, and hid everything. My father was digging a basement there, almost an underground home with a stove, our third. There were already some young vegetables peeking out of the earth in his garden.

My mother and I over the summer had become rough peasants. Our fingers were hard, with tough thick nails, permanently blackened with earth, and most interesting of all was that at the base of our nails we'd developed some sort of calluses. I noticed that Anisya had the same thing on her fingers, as did Marfutka, who didn't do anything, and even Tanya, our lady of leisure, a former nurse, had them too. Speaking of which, at this point Tanya's most frequent visitor, Vera, the shepherdess, hung herself in the forest. She wasn't actually a shepherdess anymore—all the sheep had been eaten long ago—and also she had a secret, which Anisya, who was very angry with Tanya, now told us: Vera always called for tea when she was coming into the village, but what Tanya gave Vera was some kind of medicine, which she couldn't live without, and that's why she hung herself: she had no money anymore for medicine. Vera left behind a little daughter. Anisya, who had contact with Tarutino, the neighboring village, told us that the girl was living with her grandmother, but then it emerged that the grandmother was another Marfutka, only with a drinking problem, and so the little girl, already half insane, was brought home the next day by our mother in an old baby stroller.

My mother always needed more than the rest of us, and my father was angry because the girl wet her bed and never said a word, licked her snot, didn't understand anything, and cried at night for hours. Pretty soon none of us could live or sleep for these nighttime screams, and my father went off to live in the woods. There wasn't much for it but to go and give the girl back to her failed grandmother, but just then this same grandmother, Faina, appeared and, swaying on her feet, began demanding money for the girl and the stroller. In reply my mother went inside and brought out Lena, combed, showered, barefoot but in a clean dress. At this point Lena suddenly threw herself at my mother's feet, without a word, but like a grown-up, curling herself up in a ball and putting her arms around my mother's bare ankles. Her grandmother began to cry and left without Lena and without the baby stroller—apparently, to die. She swayed on her feet as she walked and wiped her tears away with her fist—but she swayed not from drink but from hunger, as I later figured out. She didn't have any supplies—after all her daughter Vera hadn't earned anything for a long time. We ourselves mostly ate stewed grass in different forms, with plain mushroom soup being the most common.

Our little goats had been living for a while now with my father—it was safer there—and the trail to his house had almost disappeared, especially as my father never took the same path twice with his wheelbarrow, as a precaution, plotting for the future. Lena stayed with us. We would pour her off some milk, feed her berries and our mushroom soups. Everything became a lot more frightening when we thought of the coming winter. We had no flour and not a single grain of wheat; none of the farms in the area was operating—there hadn't been any gasoline or spare parts in ages, and the horses had been eaten even earlier. My father walked through the abandoned fields, picked up some grain, but others had been by before him, and he found just a little, enough for a very small sack. He thought he'd figure out how to grow wheat under the snow on the little field near his house in the woods. He asked Anisya when he should plant and sow, and she promised to tell him. She said shovels were no good, and as there weren't any plugs to be found anywhere, my father asked her to draw him a plug on a piece of paper and began, just like Robinson Crusoe, to bang together some kind of contraption. Anisya herself didn't remember exactly how it worked, even though she'd had to walk behind a cow with a plug a few times, in the old days, but my father was all aflame with his new engineering ideas and sat down to reinvent this particular wheel. He was happy with his new fate and never pined for the life of the city, where he'd left behind a great many enemies, including his parents, my grandmother and grandfather, whom I'd seen only when I was very little and who'd since been buried under the rubble of the arguments over my mom and my grandfather's apartment, may it rot, with its high ceilings and private bathroom and kitchen. We weren't fated ever to live there, and now my grandparents were probably dead. We didn't say anything to anyone when we left the city, though my father had been planning his escape for a long time. That's how we managed to have so many sacks and boxes to take with us, because all of this stuff was cheap and, once upon a time, not subject to rationing, and over the course of several years my father, a farseeing man, collected it all. My father was a former athlete, a mountain climber, and a geologist. He'd hurt his hip in an accident, and he'd long ago dreamed of escape, and here the circumstances presented themselves, and so we did, we left, while the skies were still clear. "It's a clear day in all of Spain," my father would joke, literally every morning that it was sunny out.

The summer was beautiful. Everything was blossoming, flowering. Our Lena began to talk. She'd run after us into the forest, not to pick mushrooms but to follow my mother like she was tied to her, as if it were the main task of her young life.

I taught her how to recognize edible mushrooms and berries, but it was useless—a little creature in that situation can't possibly tear herself away from grown-ups. She is saving her skin every minute of the day, and so she ran after my mother everywhere, on her short little legs, with her puffed-out stomach. She called my mother "Nanny"—where she picked up that word we had no idea; we'd never taught it to her—and she called me that, too, which was very clever, actually.

One night we heard a noise outside our door like a cat meowing and went outside to find a newborn baby wrapped in an old, greasy coat. My father, who'd grown used to Lena and sometimes even came during the day to help around the house, now simply deflated. My mother didn't like it either and immediately went over to Anisya to demand who could have done this—with the child, at night, accompanied by the quiet Lena, we marched over to Anisya's. Anisya wasn't sleeping; she had also heard the child's cries and was very worried. She said that the first refugees had already arrived in Tarutino, and that soon they'd be coming to our village too, so we should expect more guests from here on out. The infant was squealing shrilly and without interruption; he had a hard, puffed-out stomach. We invited Tanya over in the morning to have a look, and without even touching him she said he wasn't going to survive—he had the infant's disease. The child suffered, yelled, and we didn't even have a nipple for the bottle, much less any food for him. My mother dripped some water into his dried-out mouth, and he nearly choked on it. He looked like he was about four months old. My mother ran at a good clip to Tarutino, traded a precious bit of salt for a nipple, and returned full of energy, and the child drank a little bit of water from the bottle. My mother induced stool with some softening chamomile brew, and we all, including my father, darted around as fast as we could, heating the water, giving the child a warm compress. It was clear to everyone that we needed to leave the house, the plot, our whole functioning household, or else we'd be destroyed. But leaving the plot meant starving to death. At the family conference my father announced that we'd be moving to the house in the woods and that he'd stay behind for now with a rifle and the dog in the shack next door.

That night we set off with the first installment of things. The boy, whose name was now Nayden, rode atop the cart. To everyone's surprise he'd recovered, then began sucking on the goat's milk, and now rode wrapped in a sheepskin. Lena walked alongside the cart, holding onto the ropes.

At dawn we reached our new home, at which point my father immediately made a second run and then a third. He was like a cat carrying more and more of his litter in his teeth, which is to say all the many possessions he'd acquired, and now the little hut was smothered in things. That day, when all of us collapsed from exhaustion, my father set off for guard duty. At night, on his wheelbarrow, he brought back some early vegetables from the garden—potatoes, carrots, beets, and little onions. We laid this all out in the underground storage he'd created. The same night he set off again, but limped back almost immediately with an empty wheelbarrow. Gloomily he announced: "That's it!" He'd brought a can of milk for the boy. It turned out our house had been claimed by some kind of squad. They'd already posted a guard at the plot, and taken Anisya's goat. Anisya had lain in wait for my father on his escape path with that can of milk. My father was sad, but also he was pleased, since he'd once again managed to escape, and to escape with his whole family.

Now our only hope lay in my father's little plot and in the mushrooms we could find in the forest. Lena stayed in the house with the boy—we didn't take her with us to the forest now but locked her in the house to keep her out of the way. Strangely enough she sat quietly with the boy and didn't beat her fists against the door. Nayden greedily drank the potato broth, while my mother and I scoured the woods with our bags and backpacks. We no longer pickled the mushrooms but just dried them—there was hardly any salt left now. My father began digging a well, as the nearest stream was very far.

On the fifth day of our immigration we were joined by Baba Anisya. She came to us with empty hands, with just a cat on her shoulder. Her eyes looked strange. She sat for a while on the porch, holding the frightened cat on her lap, then gathered herself and went off into the woods. The cat hid under the porch. Soon Anisya came back with a whole apron's worth of mushrooms, though among them was a bright-red poisonous one. She remained sitting on the porch and didn't go into the house; we brought her out a portion of our poor mushroom soup in a can from the milk she used to give us. That evening my father took Anisya into the basement, where he'd built our third refuge, and she lay down and rested and the next day began actively scouring the forest for mushrooms. I'd go through the mushrooms she brought back, so she wouldn't poison herself. We'd dry some of them, and some we'd throw out. One time, coming home from the woods, we found all our refugees together on the porch. Anisya was rocking Nayden in her arms and telling Lena, choking on her words: "They went through everything, took everything . . . They didn't even look in on Marfutka, but they took everything of mine. They dragged the goat away by her rope." Anisya remained useful for a long time to come, took our goats out for walks, sat with Nayden and Lena until the frosts came. Then one day she lay down with the kids in the warmest place in the house, on the bunk above the stove, and from then on got up only to use the outhouse.

The winter came and covered up all the paths that might have led to us. We had mushrooms, berries (dried and boiled), potatoes from my father's plot, a whole attic filled with hay, pickled apples from abandoned gardens in the forest, even a few cans of pickled cucumbers and tomatoes. On the little field, under the snow, grew our winter crop of bread. We had our goats. We had a boy and a girl, for the continuation of the race, and a cat, who brought us mice from the forest, and a dog, Red, who didn't want to eat these mice, but whom my father would soon count on for hunting rabbits. My father was afraid to hunt with his rifle. He was even afraid to chop wood because someone might hear us. He chopped wood only during the howling snowstorms. We had a grandmother—the storehouse of the people's wisdom and knowledge.

Cold desolate space spread out around us on all sides.

One time my father turned on the radio and tried for a while to hear what was out there. Everything was silent. Either the batteries had died, or we really were the last ones left. My father's eyes shone: He'd escaped again!

If in fact we're not alone, then they'll come for us. That much is clear. But, first of all, my father has a rifle, and we have skis and a smart dog. Second of all, they won't come for a while yet. We're living and waiting, and out there, we know, someone is also living, and waiting, until our grain grows and our bread grows, and our potatoes, and our new goats—and that's when they'll come. And take everything, including me. Until then they're being fed by our plot, and Anisya's plot, and Tanya's household. Tanya is long gone, but Marfutka is still there. When we're like Marfutka, they won't touch us either.

But there's a long way to go until then. And in the meantime, of course, we're not just sitting here. My father and I have commenced work on our next refuge.

The Miracle

THERE ONCE LIVED A WOMAN WHOSE SON HANGED HIMSELF.

Which is to say, when she returned home from the night shift one morning, her boy was lying on the floor next to an overturned stool underneath a length of thin synthetic rope.

He was unconscious, but his heart still beat faintly, and so the paramedic who came with the ambulance suggested that the son wasn't really trying to hang himself.

Even though there was a note on the table: "Mom, I'm sorry. I love you."

And it was only when she'd returned home from the hospital, having held her son's hand as they rode in the ambulance, and then with him into the hospital as he lay on a stretcher, right up to the doors of the intensive care unit, where she finally had to let him go—only upon returning home did she discover that the wool sock in which she kept her savings was empty.

She kept the sock at the bottom of an old suitcase. It had contained two wedding rings, all her money, and her gold earrings set with rubies.

The poor woman then saw that the tape player—the one valuable thing she'd ever bought, because it was the only way she could get her son to return to school—was also gone.

Looking around some more, she found a number of empty bottles under the bed and in the kitchen, a mound of dirty plates in the sink, and traces of vomit in the filthy bathroom.

She knew the minute she walked in the door that there had been a party—her son was being drafted into the army and had wanted to invite his friends over, but the mother kept objecting.

And yet when she stood at the entrance to their studio apartment that morning and took in the crooked lamp, the table that had been moved, the overturned stool, and, above all, the rope and the body on the floor, all her angry thoughts left her.

Only now did she move the fallen chair aside and pull the old suitcase from underneath her bed.

It wasn't locked properly; one of the two small locks was broken.

That loose lock told her a great deal, and she opened the suitcase hopelessly, with unfeeling hands.

The wool sock was in its place, under all the clothing, but it was empty.

That sock was her last hope. She had made all sorts of plans, whether to buy a television, or to bribe someone to allow her son to take his high school exams (he'd dropped out in the middle of his senior year).

Other times she dreamed of moving to a bigger apartment, with two rooms. She'd have to scrimp and save, but she could do it, and her boy could have his own room. It wasn't easy living with him, it was true, but he was her only remaining family. The others had died, all her relatives—her parents, aunts, uncles, and husband had died young; an evil fate seemed to trail them all.

And now her boy wanted to leave her, too.

In truth he'd been talking about this for a long time. His army service was approaching inexorably, and he'd always been a quiet, gentle boy. He didn't like fighting—he always said he couldn't hurt another human being, and because of this he was often beaten up at school. There were three boys in particular who liked to pick on him. They'd laugh and say he never fought back, and they'd take everything he had in his pockets, right down to his handkerchief.

Which, incidentally, didn't mean he was above threatening his own mother when he was drunk. In fact he'd changed a great deal since he'd started hanging out with some older kids who lived in their building.

They'd taken him under their protection. He told his mother so himself, he came home one day and said, That's it, no one's going to bother me anymore. And from then on he would walk around strangely exhilarated.

That was a few years ago, when he was fourteen. That's when he began asking his mother for a tape player. The other boys would give him tapes to copy, and he couldn't admit to them that he didn't have a tape recorder of his own, so he just sat there miserably, staring at the tapes.

He'd bragged to his friends—apparently—about his tape player and now couldn't take it back. He knew his mother had some money—she was always working several jobs, saving, scrimping—but she told him pocket money would spoil him, he might even, she said, start drinking and smoking, as if they didn't already have enough problems.

He did in fact start drinking and smoking—the older kids must have paid. He also knew his mother's hiding places and would steal from her a little at a time. She was disorganized and never remembered exactly how much money she had in her stash.

One time he wouldn't stop screaming about how much he needed a tape recorder. He kept at it until he actually became ill—he had a fever, and he refused medication. He said he wanted to die.

His fever grew worse, he refused all food, and finally his mother broke down—she went out and bought him a tape recorder, the cheapest one, though it still cost a fortune.

Her son woke up right away, and he looked wide-eyed at the tape recorder. The mother was crying tears of joy, seeing how shocked he was, but then just as suddenly he lay down again, turned his back to her, and said it was the wrong model. It wasn't what he needed at all.

The next morning they crawled together to the cheap little kiosk to exchange the tape recorder for a better one. They had to pay a ton of money, again, for the upgrade—and clearly the people at the kiosk tricked them, seeing the condition the mother was in, that she was ready for anything.

After that he truly went out of control. He listened to the tape recorder day and night without a break, dubbed cassettes (which also cost money), and then soon there was the problem of a new leather jacket, designer jeans, and American sneakers.

Here the mother finally said no. After all, where would it end?

Since you're not going to school anymore, she told him, why don't you go to work like me? I'm ready for any kind of work for your sake.

He replied that he would never slave for pennies the way she did.

He refused to do what other boys in his situation did—sell newspapers or wash windshields at traffic lights. Maybe he was afraid of getting beaten up again—his mother, too, was afraid of everything, and maybe he'd grown up that way also, not having a father to set an example.

But things soon got to the point where he refused to go out in his shapeless pants and jacket, became depressed, didn't do his homework, rendering his attendance at school senseless—why show up just to be embarrassed by his teachers? He hated being lectured, couldn't stand it.

He spent more and more of his time with the neighborhood kids, his protectors, and they—thought the mother, sitting before her violated suitcase—must have drank, and smoked, and he alongside them, at their expense.

And now the time must have come when they'd reminded him of this, of their long-standing hospitality, and decided it was time to get their money back.

That must have been why he wanted to throw a going-away party, for his induction into the army. And she kept putting it off, saying there were still two months to go, they'd have time, it was early.

Of course all children know the secret places in the house where their parents hide the money.

Whereas the mother might forget. There was even a time when this Nadya, the mother, couldn't find her money sock, when she needed to buy her Vova new shoes. He was eight years old, and he pointed beneath the wardrobe—that's where she'd hidden her sock. Now he was seventeen.

†

The mother sat there, in shock, before this bankruptcy, this humiliation—someone had also scrawled obscenities on the bathroom walls, and the jars in the kitchen had been emptied of all their grains, as if the partiers were searching for something—she sat there and thought that this was the end, and there was nothing else she could do.

In the calm of the waiting room, the doctor had told her that her boy was alive and well, that they were putting him in intensive care only as a formality, but that soon he'd be transferred to the psychiatric ward.

If the psych ward declared him clinically insane, that would be his worst nightmare—because he'd secretly hoped he would someday get a car, but you can't get a license with a record of mental illness.

And in that case, too, the army wouldn't have him, and he'd continue living off of her and just tumbling further and further into the abyss.

On the other hand, if they *didn't* declare him insane—also quite likely, since he would fight against the diagnosis and insist he was just trying to scare his mother—then he'd be drafted, and that would be the end of him. He'd told her himself: I won't accept humiliations. You'll have me back in a casket soon enough. Please bury me next to Dad.

There was nothing else she could do. Nadya got through the evening, night, and morning, and then staggered over to the hospital. There she was met by the head of the psychiatric ward, a cheerful woman who told her the boy had only pretended to commit suicide, his friends were in on it too, he'd told the doctor so himself.

"But there are marks on his neck!" Nadya cried out.

"It was a very flimsy rope," answered the doctor. "He did that on purpose. He said if he'd wanted to kill himself he'd have used a thicker rope, a cord—he said you have one in the house. He remembered everything you said to the paramedics and what they looked like. He was just pretending to be unconscious."

"And the bloody foam on his mouth?" Nadya protested, but the doctor was no longer listening. She said the boy was still very upset and didn't want to face his mother after the joke he'd pulled.

"But he robbed me," Nadya wanted to say, but instead just began weeping right there in the waiting room.

"You should also seek some help," the doctor suggested in parting.

After that Nadya wandered back home again and began calling all her friends for advice.

Then she went down to the yard, where the old ladies convened on the benches, and sought their advice, too.

Somehow she couldn't help talking about what had happened, just couldn't stop her racing tongue. She stopped people on the street, people she barely knew, and insisted on telling them everything, as if she were at confession.

People had begun looking at her in a funny way, agreeing with everything she said, prompting her with questions.

She finally got help from an old woman who used to live in their building but now lived far away with her sister. She had been diagnosed (she told Nadya) with a fatal disease and had only two weeks to live, which is why she'd stayed away for a while. Before the old woman moved Nadya had occasionally brought her groceries, and the woman would tell her everything—how she'd transferred ownership of her apartment to her beloved grandson so that she could live out the last years of her life without worries about his future, and that the grandson had immediately decided to remodel the place, pulled up the floors, changed the parquet, and in the meantime moved his grandmother out to her sister's place, so as not to bother her with all the repairs. Then the grandson disappeared, and the apartment was occupied by a family no one knew, who had bought it from the grandson fair and square. So it went. Everyone in their building knew the story.

The poor exiled old woman used to go around to all the neighbors and cry about what had happened, but now she seemed to have calmed down. She didn't even mention it, said she was living well ("With your sister?" asked Nadya, but the old woman answered, "No, without my sister now," and Nadya was afraid to ask further, for fear that the sister had died), she was growing all sorts of flowers ("On your balcony?" Nadya asked, and the old woman said, "No, over my head," which seemed like a strange answer, and Nadya did not ask anything more), and in any case Nadya had to tell her own story, too, so she did.

The old woman said, "You need to find Uncle Kornil."

And that was it. She immediately began to walk away and then disappeared around the corner of her old building before Nadya could ask her anything else.

Amazed, Nadya raced around the corner and then the next corner, but the woman was gone.

There was nothing else to do. Once again Nadya called all her friends and acquaintances and anyone else she could find, to ask them about Uncle Kornil, and finally, when she was waiting in line at the post office, a woman told her that Kornil slept in the boiler room of the hospital near the metro.

Uncle Kornil was near death, the woman added, and couldn't be allowed to drink.

But the local bums who also lived in the basement wouldn't let you in to see him unless you brought them a bottle of vodka.

Nor would Kornil tell you anything unless he got a bottle, too.

What you needed to do was put down a fresh towel for a tablecloth, and shot glasses, serve the vodka, something to eat, and so on in that vein.

The woman explained in great detail where to go and what to do. She herself didn't look very well: she was pale, as if she'd just come from the hospital, and dressed all in black, with a black kerchief, but she had lovely, kind eyes.

Without even thinking, Nadya bought the vodka bottles, prepared the towel, packed everything neatly into a bag, and went off.

When she was near the hospital somebody directed her to the boiler room, the gathering spot for all local drunks. It looked like every bum in the neighborhood hung out there.

Two or three loitered near the basement door, either waiting for someone or just passing the time.

Worried they'd steal her vodka, Nadya made for the door like a tank, sweeping the drunks from the way and knocking loudly on the door. It opened just a sliver, then welcomed her fully when Nadya flashed one of her bottles from the bag. The drunks outside tried to get in behind her, and there was some commotion as she entered the basement.

She was immediately relieved of one of the bottles; the person who did so informed Nadya that Uncle Kornil was very ill and mustn't be allowed to drink under any circumstances.

He pointed her to a corner where a man lay next to an old wardrobe with its doors missing. He looked like he'd just been picked out of the trash. He lay with his arms outstretched. This was Kornil.

Nadya did as the woman at the post office had directed—she put down a fresh towel, placed a bottle of vodka atop it, cut up some bread and pickles, and also put down a little money to help Kornil with his future hangover.

Kornil lay there like a corpse, his mouth open, his forehead covered in tiny scratches, though there was a particularly large one, like a wound, right in the middle.

There were open sores on his hands.

Nadya sat there and waited, then opened the bottle and poured a large shot into the glass.

Uncle Kornil stirred, opened his eyes, crossed himself (so did Nadya), and whispered, "Nadya"—she shivered—"do you have his photograph?"

Nadya did not have a photograph of her son with her. She could have died of grief right then and there.

"Do you have anything of his?"

Nadya started rummaging through her bag. She took out a little purse, a packet of milk, and a used handkerchief. That was it.

She'd used that handkerchief to wipe away her tears on her walk home from the hospital the first time.

Nadya brought the full glass to Uncle Kornil's lips.

Uncle Kornil raised himself on an elbow, drank off the glass, chewed a pickle, and fell back down again, saying, "Give me your handkerchief."

Then, holding the handkerchief (there was a large leaking sore on his wrist), he said, "If I drink another glass, that'll be the end of me."

Growing frightened, Nadya nodded.

She was kneeling by his side, on her knees, waiting for him to speak. Her dried tears were on that handkerchief, the traces of her suffering, and in a way those were also the traces of her son—so she hoped.

"Sinner," Uncle Kornil managed, "what do you want?"

Nadya answered right away, beginning to cry: "How am I a sinner? I have no sins on my conscience."

Behind her, at the table, she heard an explosion of laughter—one of the drunks must have told a joke.

"Your grandfather killed one hundred and seven people," croaked Uncle Kornil. "And now you're about to kill me."

Nadya nodded again, wiping away tears.

Uncle Kornil went quiet.

He lay there silently; meanwhile, time was growing short.

He needed more to drink, apparently, before he would continue.

Nadya hardly knew anything about her paternal grandfather—he'd disappeared at some point. And as if there hadn't been enough wars in which people killed one another, involuntarily, without anger.

They gave you an order—and either you killed, or they killed you for disobeying the order.

"So my grandfather was a soldier," said Nadya, wounded. "But what does that have to do with the boy? What did he do? Maybe I should suffer, but why should he? Everybody killed back then—so what?"

Uncle Kornil didn't say anything; he lay there like a corpse. A drop of blood began to run down his forehead. "Oh, no," said Nadya, blanching.

She didn't have anything to wipe it away with. He was holding the handkerchief, and she couldn't very well use her skirt—she'd be walking around town in a bloody skirt.

And without the handkerchief, he wouldn't be able to say anything.

The handkerchief held the traces of her suffering and her son's suffering.

Once again laughter exploded behind her.

She turned and saw the drunks sitting around the table, laughing. They were paying no attention to her at all.

"I have nothing to hope for!" she suddenly blurted out. "You know that, Uncle Kornil."

Time passed.

The stream of blood dried on the forehead of the man on the floor.

He was unshaven, filthy, skinny; a bad smell wafted up from him; he probably hadn't stood up in days.

Empty bottles piled up in the wardrobe next to him.

Apparently this Kornil had already helped a number of people today by drinking vodka he couldn't refuse.

He was waiting for her to pour him more.

The woman had warned that without a drink he wouldn't say a thing.

Nadya poured out another glass of vodka.

Holding it up, she said: "You asked what I wanted: I want my son to be happy. That's all I want."

She stopped, imagining how this twisted Kornil would grant her wish—because happiness for her son consisted of leeching off her, drinking, partying, motorcycling.

"I want him to study. I want him to go back to school and study," she said.

She stopped again, thinking he still had two years of school left, and in the meantime she'd have to slave away at three separate jobs to feed him. And she was tired.

"He should help me," said Nadya. "He should get a job, earn some money, learn how to work hard."

But then she remembered they were going to take him into the army soon, and he'd come back very quickly in a coffin, as he'd promised.

"Let him go to college," Nadya concluded firmly. "And stay out of the army."

Then she imagined six more years (one of school, five of college) of constant torment and sleepless nights before exams. She remembered how she got whenever Vova was late from school, how she cried and yelled at him when she got summoned to school when he failed his classes or lost his textbooks or got in a fight.

"All right," Nadya said finally. "I want him to study, and work hard, and do what I say, and come home on time, and . . . no more of these friends of his! Especially the girls. And the drinking and partying. It'll end in jail, that's what. So he gets up early, leaves for work, comes back on time, cleans the house, helps me out . . ."

Then poor Nadya realized it would be best if her son were alive, healthy, a diligent student, a good worker, and never, ever at home.

When he was home it meant a racket, loud music, his stuff flung all over, phone conversations late into the night, eating standing up like a horse, accusations, demands for money followed by tears . . .

She thought of how much she'd had to endure from her one and only son, and said bitterly: "You call me a sinner, but when did I get a chance to sin? When? I don't live for myself. I live only for him . . . only for him. All I think about is how to feed and clothe him. I saved every penny, and now there's nothing left—he stole it all. Oh, and I'd like for him not to steal anymore, Uncle Kornil. No one in our family ever stole before. And I don't want him drinking. His health is bad; he has allergies, chronic bronchitis. He should go to college. After that, he should get married to a nice girl. And live with her. God bless them. It's bad enough with just him, but to have them both running around the house? And then a child? I'm tired; I've no strength left. The psychiatrist at the hospital said I should get treatment myself! But I'll help them. As for me, as for me—when can I live my life? I think only of him. I cry myself to sleep every night. What kind of sinner can I be?"

She sat back down with the glass of vodka still full in her hand. So many tears streamed from her eyes that she couldn't see anything around her.

"Work a miracle, Uncle Kornil," she begged him. "I'm not a sinner. I have no sins on my soul. Help me. Do something. I don't even know what anymore. I'm all confused."

Uncle Kornil lay motionless; he was hardly breathing. Nadya raised the glass, gingerly, to his half-open mouth, figuring how best to pour it so she wouldn't lose a single drop.

She'd have to lift his head a little—then it would work.

And it did, just as she'd planned it. With one hand she held up Uncle Kornil's head, and with the other she began carefully moving the glass to his thin, desiccated lips.

All the while she was crying and pleading that her wishes be fulfilled, though it wasn't clear anymore what they were.

"Now, now," she said soothingly. "We'll just drink this and everything will be fine."

At that moment his eyes shot open, like a dead man's— Nadya knew the look well, the one that stared hard into a dark corner as if all the truth of the world were there.

Nadya could see that her wishes were not coming true, that Kornil was going to die at any moment, without having done a thing.

The vodka was her last hope.

If she could just pour this last glass into him, maybe he would come alive for a moment. Then he could die if he wanted. He'd said himself that one more glass and he was done for.

But that glass: she hadn't got it in yet!

How could this be? Uncle Kornil had promised!

He'd helped everyone else, but not her. Look at all those empty bottles in the wardrobe from all the people he'd helped.

At this point she heard the men behind her start speaking all at once.

"Ah, here's Andreevna, Andreevna's here. Open up for Andreevna! Kornil, look, your mom's here. She sensed there was a bottle open, oh, she sensed it!" And they laughed.

A female profile flitted past the window outside.

Nadya froze in confusion, the glass still in her hand.

She had to finish this quickly, before Uncle Kornil's mom appeared.

"It's always like that," thought Nadya bitterly. "Everyone else manages, but I can't."

She was still holding the heavy hand of the dying man, whose wide-open eyes continued to stare at the ceiling.

"Uncle Kornil!" Nadya called to him. "Uncle Kornil, here, drink this!"

His mouth was wide open now, his jaw hanging down loosely.

Someone was knocking at the door, and someone was already moving to open it.

"I just have to keep from spilling it," Nadya thought hysterically, "otherwise it's all over for me."

She was convinced that if she could keep from spilling the vodka, all her wishes would come true. This life of torture would end. She raised Kornil's head to a better angle.

"That's good now," she was saying, again bringing the glass to Kornil's lips. "Now let's drink. Yum."

Just the way she'd fed her son milk when he was little.

This was in the countryside, where they'd lived when Vova was a baby, and her husband would come out on weekends.

Vovochka was always opening his mouth, with his two little teeth, so awkwardly, and the milk would spill.

Here the door slammed, and a loud drunk female voice called out, "What're you drinking, my low-life friends?"

"It's his mother," Nadya thought in terror. "I didn't make it. I'm too late."

The glass trembled in her hand.

The mother was going to come over and put an end to this.

"Andreevna, you better start collecting for a coffin," someone said. "Your Kornil is being fed his last one over there."

"What's he need a coffin for?" the woman answered heartily. "We'll sell his body to the med school. First round's on him!"

She was met with a roar of approving laughter.

"You, over there—Nadya, right?" said the woman without looking over. "Keep working on that bastard. Go ahead. He'll die, oh he'll die all right. Just open his trap and shove that last one down."

"How does she know my name?" thought Nadya, terrified.

"Give it a good push," the woman went on. "Finish him off. He knew you'd come, he did. He's had enough of it here. Everyone loves him; they all bring him something to drink. He can't refuse—there would be hurt feelings, and he just can't hurt anyone's feelings. He's like that."

The men all brayed happily. Nadya was afraid to turn around. From what she could tell, the woman had sat down at the table, and they were pouring her a glass. "He was just waiting for her," someone said. " 'My cup will runneth over,' he said."

Nadya was no longer thinking. Both her hands shook.

"Go ahead, ask him—he'll do everything!" yelled the mother. "He did everything for everyone. He worked miracles. He gave sight to the blind. He healed the lame. He even brought this one Jew, Lazar Moiseivich, back from the dead. This Lazar's family had already started suing one another over the inheritance—that's how dead he was! He was resurrected, and they all got mad at Kornil. 'Who asked you?' they said. Actually, it was his second wife who asked him to do it. She'd lived with him after his first wife died, raised his children. When he died, the children sued her right away for the apartment, said she should get out or pay them off—there were two of them. So this wife found Kornil, put two bottles before him. Lazar was resurrected; he didn't know what hit him.

"Then Kornil raised a legless man. His mother came here, said she didn't know what to do, her son was rotting away before her eyes. So Kornil gives him legs, and what does the son do? He starts drinking just like before, chasing his mother around the apartment with a knife in his hand. She runs back here and says: Put him down again!"

The men all laughed terribly at that one.

The mother took a shot of vodka, coughed, and went on.

"Whatever you wish for, that's what will happen, Nadya—believe me. Give him the drink—that's what you're here for. He chose you to do it. Remember the woman at the post office? That was me. He told me: Nadya is ready for anything. She has what it takes. She needs to resolve the Vova situation once and for all. Now, don't you worry, Nadya. You have a tough time with your son—well, my son has a tough time, too. He really shouldn't have come down this time—he really shouldn't. And now he's waiting for someone to see him off. He can't just go back himself—that's not allowed. He needs someone to help him."

Nadya wasn't listening. She looked at Uncle Kornil, whose head still lay on her arm, and nodded, carefully setting the glass of vodka down on the towel.

"No offense," she said finally, "but we'll manage on our own. Your son here is very sick—you should get him to a hospital. And not give him anything more to drink. Really, what's the matter with you? You're his mother, after all. He's dying as we speak. My husband died on my arm—I know what I'm talking about." And, to punctuate this speech, she gave the glass a little poke, and it tottered and fell. The vodka spilled out on the floor, and everything was suddenly enshrouded in fog.

✝

Nadya found herself on the street, walking home. She felt a little lightheaded. Her mind was clear and free of all burdens.

She walked lightly and happily, not crying, not thinking about the future, not worrying about anything.

As though she'd passed the hardest test of her life.

Requiems

The God Poseidon

ONE TIME WHILE VACATIONING BY THE SEA I RAN INTO MY friend Nina, a single mother in middle age. Nina invited me to her house, and there I saw strange things. The entrance, for example, had cathedral ceilings and a marble stairwell. Then the apartment itself—dominated by dark wood and vermilion tapestries, its floor covered with a plush gray carpet. It looked magnificent, like something you'd see photographed in the magazine *L'Art de Decoration*, and the bath especially was impressive, the floor carpeted in gray, with mirrors and a light blue china wash basin—it was simply a dream! I could hardly believe my eyes. Meanwhile, Nina, who had kept her look of eternal suffering and passivity, led me into the bedroom with its three open doors, a little dark but still very elegant, with a surprising number of unmade beds. "Did you get married?" I asked Nina, but she just walked out one of the doors with a look of concern, like a busy housewife but somehow not touching anything. The bedroom was glorious—like in a hotel—with enormous closets, twelve feet long, filled with gowns. How did all these riches fall on poor

83

Nina, who'd never even had decent underwear, who had one ancient coat for every season and three dresses, all told? She got married—but here? This wild place where no one lives, where people just wait in the seaside emptiness for summer, when they can let their rooms to strangers? But how could she rent this house with its stairwells, corridors, arches . . . and what's more, I happened to open a wrong door and found myself in a white-marble courtyard, where a teacher was leading schoolkids on a field trip.

All right, so she got married, but it turned out she'd also traded her small one-room apartment in Moscow, where she'd been getting by with her teenage son, for this glorious apartment, with all the furniture and even bedsheets! Which is to say, the owners didn't touch anything—they just left—except in fact they hadn't left at all, which is why Nina looked so glum, I think. The extra beds in the room were for the landlady and her son, a quiet young fisherman with puffy cheeks. The landlady still bustled around the house, and in fact we sat down to dinner under her patronage. She behaved exactly as if she were a quiet and docile mother-in-law and Nina her honored daughter, for whom she bent and toiled in the house, all the while maintaining her position as the head of the household and not allowing Nina close to anything, in fact.

It turned out the woman had exchanged apartments with Nina, and Nina had left her job at the newspaper and moved here, planning to write about this new place, about the sea, which she'd always loved—she'd always had a weakness for anything to do with it—but in the meantime she was just moping around this new place, which the owner hadn't yet left. Formally everything was in order—Nina had all the papers, and she and her son owned the house and lived there—but the old landlady had stayed there all winter, with her son, and they hadn't mentioned leaving. Nina had always been a disorganized person who let things go; thus her leave from the newspaper to go "freelance" and the apparent total unraveling of her life. Nina accepted things here as she found them. She ate, drank, walked out to the sea; her son attended the local school, which was quite good; and they didn't need any money, since every day the young fisherman would bring the fruits of the sea home to them.

"Who is he?" I asked, and Nina, without any hesitation, answered that he was the son of Poseidon, god of the sea, that he could live and breathe underwater, that he brought home literally everything from there, that he walked sometimes on the floor of the ocean to other countries, and brought home shells and jewels, and everything else for the house and the family.

Meanwhile Poseidon's old wife, who had for some reason taken poor Nina under her wing, sat at the head of the table, underneath the tall window, and kept feeding and feeding us, and as I ate I kept thinking of that gorgeous hotel-like bedroom with its four beds and their sheets as white as sea foam—and I was thinking Nina was right: you should let things take their course, not fight the current, just lay down your oars and you will breathe underwater, and the god of the sea will take you in and set you up in a lovely apartment. Because, returning home to Moscow, I learned that Nina hadn't moved anywhere, in fact, but had drowned with her teenage son in a well-known ferry accident not far from the spot where I had just been, not suspecting anything.

My Love

GIVEN TIME HIS DREAMS MIGHT HAVE COME TRUE, AND HE might have found himself with the woman he loved, but the road was too long and it brought him nowhere. All he had with him that barren time was a page from a magazine, with a photograph of the woman he loved, and in fact only a few people from work knew it was her. It was just a pair of legs, that was all, a little chubby at that, bare, in heels; she herself had immediately recognized it—by her purse, and the hem of her dress. How was she to know that just her lower half was being photographed?—the photographer had rushed out into the street and taken a few quick snapshots, but they published only the hem and the legs. He—this man—kept the photograph tacked up over his desk at home, and his wife never brought it up with him, though she was a strict woman and ran the entire household, including her mother, and her children, and even her distant relatives and students. On the other hand, she was also a kind, generous, hospitable woman—she just didn't give any slack to the children, and also her meek mother lived with them, lay on the cot, read aloud to her little grandkids while she still could, and enjoyed the warmth, peace, the television, and then afterward she spent a long time dying, also meekly, barely alive now, and went without much fuss in the end.

As for him, having buried his mother-in-law, he began waiting patiently for his wife to die as well. For some reason he knew that she would go first and set him free, and he began to prepare for this event very actively: he was healthy and athletic, went running in the mornings, even toyed with weights, kept a strict diet, and in the meantime managed to work like a bull, was promoted to the head of his department, traveled abroad—and waited. His chosen one, the pretty plump little blonde, every man's dream (she looked like Marilyn Monroe), worked in the same place as he did and sometimes came along on business trips—and that's when their real lives would begin. Restaurants, hotels, strolling and shopping, tours and talks. How lonely he felt on those nights when he had to descend from heaven back into his hell, into the warm, poor nest where his graceless, cramped home life slowly bubbled, where his children got sick, went crazy, ran around like maniacs, not allowing him to concentrate, so he had to quiet them down, and sometimes this meant strapping them with his belt, after which he felt even more insulted and humiliated. His wife screamed at the kids too—she had no time for anything, she could barely turn around in that apartment, in which, as in any decent household, they also had a dog and a cat, and the cat would howl all through the night when she was in heat, and the little dog would bark every time the elevator reached their floor. The nights were the worst: he would lie in his bed and fall into cheerless dreaming of the warmth, calm, and beauty that emanated from his forbidden friend on their trips abroad. When they weren't together, she too was hounded by life: her husband and her mother-in-law literally hung on her neck, her mother-in-law forcing her to scrub the apartment every Saturday, to the point where she was scrubbing the tiles in the bath with ammonium! Her husband would get drunk and forbid her to go to office parties, birthdays, or to anything else, always made trouble before her business trips, suspected her of everything—together he and the mother-in-law were crushing her like Scylla and Charybdis, and what is more they fought each other, the husband and his mother. The mother-in-law was always demanding to know of the pretty blonde why her husband drank so much and ate so little—even that was her fault! The girl would complain about it at work, but only obliquely; she was discreet and never threw it all up in his face the way his wife would. Sometimes you find a woman like that, the lonely husband would think as he tossed in his bed, while on the other side of the wall his children cried and whimpered in their sleep, and his wife snored heavily because of her heart problem, growing older and more loving with each day. Now here was something the mind could never grasp: how she, a dried-up old woman past forty, so loved and took such care of him! It seemed as though she could never quite believe that this elegant man, with his handsomely graying whiskers, could be her husband; in fact she was too shy to accompany him anywhere. She tailored her uniformly plain dresses herself, long and baggy, the better to hide her girth and the runs in her panty hose—there was never enough money to buy new ones. This was known as "dressing modestly and tastefully" by the many guests and relatives who came crowding in during all the holidays, devouring her pies, cakes, and salads—they were all her guests, not his, her classmates, her colleagues, her relatives—they remembered her young, pretty, with cute dimples and a long thick braid, and they didn't even notice that she was already someone else, that she had dimmed.

In fact she'd long since disposed of her braid and her dimples, and instead toiled for her husband and her mother, raised the children, loyally ran for him, her lord and master, to the fresh food market, didn't have time for anything, and yet miraculously was always everywhere on time (she tried so hard to be organized)—and naturally at night, having put everyone to bed, she'd sit in the kitchen with her books, or work for extra cash, or else prepare her classes. Coming home from work she'd tell stories about her students, and once in a while she'd cook a whole bucketful of meatballs and a bucketful of kasha, and her students would come, they'd bring flowers and even make a bit of noise; shyly, they'd eat up everything and then entertain her with their clumsy singing. But this was only if the man of the house was away; otherwise, it was out of the question.

When the kids were born, a boy and a girl, even then her first thought had been of her husband: making sure he had breakfast before work, and a warm dinner after work, and that she was available to listen to everything he wanted to tell her. There was only one interruption, when her mother started dying, and then continued to die for three years: then everything was cast aside and just kind of hobbled along, it wasn't clear how, and the man of the house was reduced to self-service in the kitchen, to eating breakfast alone, whatever had been left out for him, and eating supper by himself, and then withdrawing into his room as gloomy as a storm cloud, but still he was there to carry the coffin, and was indistinguishable in his genuine grief from everyone else. After the funeral the grandmother's room remained empty, closed— no one had the strength to do anything about it. And in fact the wife quietly resisted doing anything, slept in the big room with the kids, or rather sat as always in the kitchen; sleep had abandoned her.

For the husband this was a difficult time, too: his love began complaining, demanding a real, independent, family life; she refused to accompany him anymore to friends' empty apartments during lunch, and she went even further: she started flirting with the men in adjacent offices and in the cafeteria. And the men, sensing that she'd "let down her guard," as they put it, beat a path to her door, and her telephone rang off the hook, and someone came to pick her up in a car, and so on. Our husband endured the torments of hell—love and duty tore him apart. He took a hard line with his girlfriend (though he did, occasionally, find solace in crying on her shoulder). What could he do? The wife, for all her desperation and grief, nonetheless noticed that her husband had somehow dried up, that his eyes had gone dangerously blank and that he was just drifting away. She roused herself, quickly fixed up her mother's room and moved in there with the kids, and the main room again became a meeting place for guests, and talks, and little parties, and the husband would greet the guests as the father of beautiful children and the head of a household (and not as an abandoned homeless dog), and as a beloved, worshipped husband (not just as anyone). Now he received his breakfast before everyone else, and suddenly a few new dresses were sewn from cheap cotton, and on Sundays the wife began taking the kids away for long excursions—to the park, the circus, the planetarium. But in the husband's room the photograph still hung, with its skirt, its bare chubby legs, and the heels: he wasn't giving up.

Finally thunder shook them all. The husband of the blonde—"our husband," as the illicit couple called him—came apart at the seams, completely lost it, chased the blonde around the apartment with an ax. She locked herself in the bathroom until evening, then somehow slipped out of the house, called our hero from a pay phone, and he ran to meet her and didn't come back until it was almost morning. A few hours later he was again awoken by a terrible—as all news is that comes at dawn—phone call: the husband's mother had found him hanging in the doorway from a rope. Of course the new widow spent the next month with some caring friends who took pity on her, and meanwhile our husband couldn't bring himself to invite her over, and eventually the friends who had taken her in had to terminate the blonde's stay, she was just too pretty, pale and in mourning, so that the husband of the house had begun to experience toward the blonde certain feelings of Platonic Friendship and Sympathy, which are much more dangerous than our plain human filth, in and out, in and out, and it's over. The man's wife kicked her out.

It took a while, but eventually things settled down. The blonde was given her own apartment, and someone decided he wanted to buy the old run-down place where the mother-in-law still lived. He convinced the mother-in-law to trade it for a smaller place, closer to her niece, and the blonde got a place farther out and less attractive but still her own, and here our husband, our hero, finally had to choose once and for all, yes or no, and start remodeling the place, and find furniture, fix the wiring, winterize the windows, etc., in his girlfriend's new apartment. Instead, he began setting up his own household with renewed vigor, wallpapered the main room with the help of the kids, once again started exercising, pouring cold water on himself in the mornings, running, and he began looking after the kids, drilling them, because they'd grown up and were getting in the way, was the thing. With the blonde he remained in the role of counselor and visitor. She took care of everything herself—that occupied her time. She asked for advice, showed him floor plans, and already there was someone else coming around—he had a car, he brought her hard-to-get tiles for the bathroom and even harder-to-get kitchen furniture. The blonde assessed the situation correctly and kept everyone in sight, faced with the prospect of loneliness.

The photo still hung above his desk, and he already had an assigned day for visiting the blonde—he had, incidentally, left the institute where they'd worked, his relations with it having soured when she, the blonde, was supposed to be promoted and get a raise but was turned down because the others complained. He left in protest and promised to bring her with him eventually, whereas his wife didn't understand anything and just shone with relief, and there was a party in the house, and they baked pies, because the husband had finally left Her, though the photo still hung in its place.

He did well at his new job, and the little kids grew up, athletic and tall, well-mannered, the way kids can be when they're in a family that worships its father, strengthened by the love and servitude of its self-effacing mother. The word of the father was law, and that's how they walked, in order: the father first, then the children shoulder to shoulder, and then behind them, a bundle of a mother, directing the family from a distance, as with a remote control. It was a joy to see them, though the photo of the legs was still there.

The mother of the house waited until the boy, the younger one, entered college, and then surrendered entirely, just as her mother had done. Standing in the kitchen one evening, she collapsed in front of everyone, began to choke and continued choking for three nights in the hospital. The family, disciplined and hardworking, instantly regrouped, set up a watch in shifts, and old friends and relatives came to help, as well as her long-ago and still loyal students. And from the other side, from inevitable death and oblivion, the husband rescued his wife. By the time they brought her home she was already a shriveled old lady. The only thing she could move was her right hand, and only a little. She would make sounds with her lips that no one could understand, and often, often, a tear would come running out of her eye. It was as though she were apologizing with her whole being for this state of things, apologizing for her entire former life, for not being able to create anything for her demigod, and in the end making herself a cripple. In time the members of the household grew used to their heavy burden, though sometimes they'd grow frustrated and yell at one another—all those bedpans, and daily baths, and bed sores, and then thoughts, involuntary thoughts, about how long this might go on, how many years, this animal or even vegetable state—they suffered these thoughts. But the husband seemed to calm down suddenly: his soul became anchored, and all his movements around his wife were soft, patient, his voice gentle. The kids still sometimes screamed at each other and at their mother. They had their own uncertainties—they were losing her, their foundation and their pillar—and they became weak, unsteady parents to her. They felt that something was wrong, that they didn't have a future, or rather that they did, but that it was awful. The kids blamed each other, said everything to each other, and, oh God, in front of their mother! But their devotion did not diminish. Their mother lay there clean and fresh, and they put a little radio transmitter next to her pillow and sometimes they'd read aloud to her, but still she often cried, for no reason at all, it seemed, and would try to say something with just vowel sounds, without using her tongue.

On the night she died and they took her away, her husband collapsed, and in his sleep he heard her—she was there, and she lay her head down on the pillow next to him and said, "My love." And after that he slept happily, and at the funeral he was calm and dignified, though he'd lost a great deal of weight, and was honest and upright, and at the wake, when everyone had gathered at his apartment, he told them all that

she had come to him and called him "My love." And everyone froze, because they knew what he said was true—and the
photograph no longer hung over his desk. It had disappeared
from his life. It had all evaporated—just ceased to be interesting at some point—and suddenly, while still at the table,
the husband began showing everyone the pale little family
photos of his wife and kids—of all those excursions they'd
taken without him, all their fatherless entertainments that
were so poor but so happy, in the parks and the planetariums
to which she'd brought the children when she tried to make
a life for them on the tiny island, the only one still left her,
where she shielded the children with herself, while towering
over everything was that photo from the magazine. But the
photo was gone now, everything was fine, and she'd managed
to say to him, "My love"—without words, already dead, but
she had done it.

The Fountain House

THERE ONCE LIVED A GIRL WHO WAS KILLED, THEN BROUGHT
back to life. That is, her parents were told that the girl was
dead, but they couldn't have the body (they had all been rid-
ing the bus together; the girl was standing up front at the
time of the explosion, and her parents were sitting behind
her). The girl was just fifteen, and she was thrown back by
the blast.

While they waited for the ambulance, and while the dead
were separated from the wounded, the father held his daughter in his arms, though it was clear by then that she was dead;
the doctor on the scene confirmed this. But they still had to
take the girl away, and the parents climbed into the ambulance with their girl and rode with her to the morgue.

She seemed to be alive, as she lay on the stretcher, but she
had no pulse, nor was she breathing. Her parents were told
to go home, but they wouldn't—they wanted to wait for the
body, though there were still some necessary procedures to
be done, namely the autopsy and determination of the cause
of death.

But the father, who was mad with grief, and who was also a deeply religious man, decided to steal his little daughter. He took his wife, who was barely conscious, home, endured a conversation with his mother-in-law, woke up their neighbor, who was a nurse, and borrowed a white hospital robe. Then he took all the money they had in the house and went to the nearest hospital, where he hired an empty ambulance (it was two in the morning), and with a stretcher and a young paramedic, whom he bribed, drove to the hospital where they were keeping his daughter, walked past the guard down the stairs to the basement corridor, and entered the morgue. There was no one there. Quickly he found his daughter and together with the paramedic put her on their stretcher, called down the service elevator, and took her to the third floor, to the intensive care unit. The father had studied the layout of the hospital earlier, while they waited for the body.

He let the paramedic go. After a brief negotiation with the doctor on duty, money changed hands, and the doctor admitted the girl to the intensive care unit.

Since the girl was not accompanied by a medical history, the doctor probably decided that the parents had hired an ambulance on their own and brought the girl to the nearest hospital. The doctor could see perfectly well that the girl was dead, but he badly needed the money: his wife had just given birth (also to a daughter), and all his nerves were on edge. His mother hated his wife, and they took turns crying, and the child also cried, and now on top of all this he had of late been assigned exclusively night shifts. He desperately needed money for an apartment. The sum that this (clearly insane) father had offered him to revive his dead princess was enough for half a year's rent.

This is why the doctor began to work on the girl as if she were still alive, but he did request that the father change into hospital clothing and lie down on the cot next to his daughter, since this apparently sick man was determined not to leave her side.

The girl lay there as white as marble; she was beautiful. The father, sitting on his cot, stared at her like a madman. One of his eyes seemed out of focus, and it was only with difficulty in fact that he was able to open his eyes at all.

The doctor, having observed this for a while, asked the nurse to administer a cardiogram, and then quickly gave his new patient a shot of tranquilizer. The father fell asleep. The girl continued to lie there like Sleeping Beauty, hooked up to her various machines. The doctor fussed around her, doing all he could, though there was no longer anyone watching him with that crazy unfocused eye. In truth, this young doctor was himself a fanatic of his profession—there was nothing more important to him than a difficult case, than a sick person, no matter who it was, on the brink of death.

The father slept, and in his dream he met his daughter—he went to visit her, as he used to visit her at summer camp. He prepared some food, just one sandwich, and that was all. He got on the bus—again it was a bus—on a fine summer evening, somewhere near the Sokol metro station, and rode it to the paradisial spot where his daughter was staying. In the fields, among soft green hills, he found an enormous gray house with arches reaching to the sky, and when he walked past these giant gates into the garden, there, in an emerald clearing, he saw a fountain, as tall as the house, with one tight stream that cascaded at the top into a glistening crown. The sun was setting slowly in the distance, and the father walked happily across the lawn to the entrance to the right of the gate, and took the stairs up to a high floor. His daughter seemed a little embarrassed when she greeted him, as if he'd interrupted her. She stood there, looking away from him—as if she had her own, private life here that had nothing to do with him anymore, a life that was none of his business.

The place was enormous, with high ceilings and wide windows, and it faced south, into the shade and the fountain, which was illuminated by the setting sun. The fountain's stream rose even higher than the windows.

"I brought you a sandwich, the kind you like," said the father.

He went over to the table by the window, put his little package down, paused for a moment, and then unwrapped it. There lay his sandwich, with its two pieces of cheap black bread. He wanted to show his daughter that there was a patty inside, and so he moved the bread pieces apart. But inside he saw—and right away he knew what it was—a raw human heart. The father was terrified that the heart had not been cooked, that the sandwich was inedible, and quickly wrapped the sandwich back up. Turning to his daughter he said awkwardly: "I mixed up the sandwiches. I'll bring you another."

But his daughter now came over and began looking at the sandwich with a strange expression on her face. The father tried to hide the little bag in his pocket and press his hands over it, so his daughter couldn't take it.

She stood next to him, with her head down, and reached out her hand: "Give me the sandwich, Papa. I'm really hungry."

"You can't eat this filth."

"Give it to me," she said ponderously.

She was reaching her hand toward his pocket—her arm was amazingly long all of a sudden—and the father understood that if his daughter ate this sandwich, she would die.

Turning away, he took out the sandwich and quickly ate the raw heart himself. Immediately his mouth filled with blood. He ate the black bread with the blood.

"And now I will die," he thought. "I'm glad at least that I will go first."

"Can you hear me? Open your eyes!" someone said.

The father opened his eyes with difficulty and saw, as through a fog, the doctor's blurry face.

"I can hear you," he said.

"What's your blood type?"

"The same as my daughter's."

"Are you sure?"

"I'm sure."

They carted him away, tied off his left arm, and stuck a needle in it.

"How is she?" asked the father.

"In what sense?" said the doctor, concentrating on his work.

"Is she alive?"

"What d'you think?" the doctor grumbled.

"She's alive?"

"Lie down, lie down," the wonderful doctor insisted.

The father lay there—nearby he could hear someone's heavy breathing—and began to cry.

†

Then they were working on him, and he was carted off again, and again he was surrounded by green trees, but this time he was woken by a noise: his daughter, on the cot next to him, was breathing in a terribly screechy way, as if she couldn't get enough air. Her father watched her. Her face was white, her mouth open. A tube carried blood from his arm to hers. He felt relieved, and tried to hurry the flow of blood—he wanted all of it to pour into his child. He wanted to die so that she could live.

Once again he found himself inside the apartment in the enormous gray house. His daughter wasn't there. Quietly he went to look for her, and searched in all the corners of the dazzling apartment with its many windows, but he could find no living being. He sat on the sofa, then lay down on it. He felt quietly content, as if his daughter were already off living somewhere on her own, in comfort and joy, and he could afford to take a break. He began (in his dream) to fall asleep, and here his daughter suddenly appeared. She stepped like a whirlwind into the room, and soon turned into a spinning column, a tornado, howling, shaking everything around her, and then sunk her nails into the bend in his right arm, under the skin.

He felt a sharp pain, yelled out in terror, and opened his eyes. The doctor had just given him a shot to his right arm.

His girl lay next to him, breathing heavily, but no longer making that awful screeching noise. The father raised himself up on an elbow, saw that his left arm was already free of the tourniquet, and bandaged, and turned to the doctor.

"Doctor, I need to make a phone call."

"What phone call?" the doctor answered. "It's too early for phone calls. You stay still, or else I'm going to start losing you, too . . ."

But before leaving he gave the father his cell phone, and the father called home. No one answered. His wife and mother-in-law must have woken up early and gone to the morgue and now must be running around, confused, not knowing where their daughter's body had gone.

$\dagger$

The girl was already better, though she had not yet regained consciousness. The father tried to stay near her in intensive care, pretending that he was himself dying. The night doctor had left already, and the poor father had no money anymore, but they gave him a cardiogram and kept him in intensive care—apparently the night doctor had managed to speak with someone. Either that or there really was something wrong with his heart.

The father considered what to do. He couldn't go downstairs. They wouldn't let him call. Everyone was a stranger, and they were all busy. He thought about what his two women must be going through now, his "girls," as he called them—

his wife and mother-in-law. His heart was in great pain. They had put him on a drip, just like his daughter.

He fell asleep, and when he awoke, his daughter was no longer there.

"Nurse, where is the girl who was here before?" he said.

"What's it to you?"

"I'm her father, that's what. Where is she?"

"They took her into the operating room. Don't worry, and don't get up. You can't yet."

"What's wrong with her?"

"I don't know."

"Dear nurse, please call the doctor!"

"They're all busy."

An old man was moaning nearby. Next door a resident was putting an old lady through some procedures, all the while addressing her loudly and jocularly, like a village idiot: "Well, grandma, how about some soup?" Pause. "What kind of soup do we like?"

"Mm," the old woman groaned in a nonhuman, metallic voice.

"How about some mushroom soup?" Pause. "With some mushrooms, eh? Have you tried the mushroom soup?"

Suddenly the old woman answered in her deep metallic bass: "Mushrooms—with macaroni."

"There you go!" the resident cried out.

The father lay there, thinking they were operating on his daughter. Somewhere his wife was waiting, half-mad with grief, his mother-in-law next to her, fretting . . . A young doctor checked in on him, gave him another shot, and he fell asleep again.

In the evening he got up and, barefoot, just as he was, in his hospital gown, walked out. He reached the stairs unnoticed and began descending the cold stone steps. He went down to the basement hallway and followed the arrows to the morgue. Here some person in a white robe called out to him:

"What are you doing here, patient?"

"I'm from the morgue," replied the father. "I got lost."

"What do you mean, from the morgue?"

"I left, but my documents are still there. I want to go back, but I can't find it."

"I haven't the faintest idea what you're saying," said the white robe, taking him by the arm and escorting him down the corridor. And then finally he asked: "You what? You got up?"

"I came to life, and there was no one around, so I started walking, and then I decided I should come back, so they could note that I was leaving."

"Wonderful!" said his escort.

They reached the morgue, but there they were greeted by the curses of the morgue attendant on duty. The father heard him out and said: "My daughter is here, too. She was supposed to come here after her operation." He told the man his name.

"I tell you she's not here, she's not here! They're all driving me crazy! They were looking for her this morning! She's not here! They're driving everyone nuts! And this one's a mental patient! Did you run off from a nuthouse, eh? Where'd he come from?"

"He was wandering around the hallway," the white robe answered.

"We should call the guard in," said the attendant and started cursing again.

"Let me call home," said the father. "I just remembered—I was in intensive care on the third floor. My memory is all confused; I came here after the explosion on Tverskaya."

Here the white robes went quiet. The explosion on the bus on Tverskaya had happened the day before. They took him, shivering and barefoot, to a desk with a telephone.

His wife picked up and immediately burst into tears.

"You! *You!* Where have you been! They took her body, we don't know where! And you're running around! There's no money in the house! We don't even have enough for a taxi! Did you take all the money?"

"I was—I was unconscious. I ended up in the hospital, in intensive care."

"Which one, where?"

"The same one where she was."

"Where is she? *Where?*" His wife howled.

"I don't know. I don't know. I'm all undressed—bring me my things. I'm standing here in the morgue, I'm barefoot. Which hospital is this?" he asked the white robe.

"How'd you end up there? I don't understand," his wife said, still weeping.

He handed the phone to the white robe, who calmly spoke the address into it, as if nothing at all strange was happening, and then hung up.

The morgue attendant brought him a robe and some old, ragged slippers—he took pity finally on this rare living person to enter his department—and directed him to the guard post at the hospital entrance.

His wife and mother-in-law arrived there with identically puffed-up, aged faces. They dressed the father, put shoes on him, hugged him, and finally heard him out, crying happily, and then all together they sat in the waiting room, because they were told that the girl had made it through her operation and was recovering, and that her condition was no longer critical.

Two weeks later she was up again walking. The father walked with her through the hospital corridors, repeating the whole time that she'd been alive after the explosion, she was just in shock, just in shock. No one noticed, but he knew right away.

He kept quiet about the raw human heart he'd had to eat. It was in a dream, though, that it happened, and dreams don't count.

The Shadow Life

She's a tall, grown-up, married woman now, but she was once an orphan living with her grandmother, who had taken her in when the girl's mother disappeared. That happens sometimes—a person will just disappear. Her father had disappeared earlier, when the girl was just five. She hadn't been allowed to go to the funeral, and so she thought he'd simply vanished, and worried very much that the same would happen to her mother. The girl clung to her mother whenever she tried to go out at night, though she never cried—her mother didn't spoil her. She was a quiet, well-behaved girl, and she remained that way until one day her mother really did vanish, just as the girl had feared, and, only nine years old, the girl spent the night alone, using her mother's bathrobe for a blanket. In the morning she washed up and went to school just as she was, in the same dress as the day before. The neighbors noticed something wrong on the third day, when the girl stopped going to school. Strange sounds came from her apartment, like someone laughing, and no cooking smells came from the kitchen, and no one—not the girl, not the girl's mom—came in or out. One of the neighbors got the girl—her name was Zhenya—to admit that she hadn't eaten in two days and that her mother was gone. The neighbors sprang into action, composed a telegraph to the girl's grandmother, and so in the middle of winter the grandmother came to their little town on the River Oka and took her granddaughter away to the quiet seaside town where she lived.

The road was familiar—Zhenya had come to visit her grandmother during all her school vacations—but there was no vacation now. They couldn't find out anything about her mother—not a single trace. The girl's grandmother told her that her mother had always fought for truth, had never stolen, even while everyone around her was stealing. She worked in a kindergarten, and the grandmother thought she'd gone to Moscow to seek justice—she had just been fired from her job—and had probably been locked up in a mental hospital. That happened sometimes, according to the grandmother.

✝

Zhenya grew up a quiet and good-looking girl, and even began attending a teachers' college in a nearby town. She studied hard and was known and liked throughout her dorm for the fact that whenever she received a package from her grandmother, with vegetables, bacon, and dried fruits, she'd put it out on the table and share it with everyone. Afterward they'd go hungry again, but all together. Zhenya had never been spoiled by her mother and grandmother, and so she didn't complain about life in the dorm.

She soon found a boyfriend, a construction worker—a foreman, even—named Sasha who would take her on the train out to the countryside during the spring and read her his homemade poems—though unfortunately, as it turned out, he was married.

The wife learned about Zhenya and sought her out in the dorm, took her outside, and told her that she was married to Sasha, and that they had two children, though at the moment they lived apart because Sasha had a sexually transmitted disease and was being treated for it. The wife was being treated for it too, though *where* Sasha had picked up this disease was the question, said the wife, and then looked at Zhenya with hatred. They were sitting in the little park outside Zhenya's dorm. "As for you," the wife concluded, "you should be shot like a sick dog, the way you're spreading that disease."

The penniless student had no one to ask for advice. She was afraid to go to the university clinic (everyone would find out!), but, luckily, while wandering around the market one day she saw a sign for VENEREAL DISEASE TREATMENT. An old woman doctor met her inside, but Zhenya had no money, and without money the old doctor wouldn't even hear her out. So Zhenya removed her earrings, the only possession she still had from her mother. The doctor took the earrings, examined Zhenya, and announced that they'd have to run some tests. The tests came back negative. Zhenya had managed to avoid being infected; either that or Sasha's wife had been lying. But Sasha no longer came by, and Zhenya began to see that things weren't so simple among people, that there existed a whole other secret, stubbornly flourishing animal side of life, where revolting, horrible things collected, and maybe her mother had been killed, thought the now grown-up (eighteen-year-old) Zhenya: after all, her mother had been young still and might have fallen into that shadow life, from which so many people never return.

Also that summer, back home, something bad happened to Zhenya. The week before, two bodies had been found at the town dump. They were women, and they had been slashed and mutilated, their arms twisted behind them like dried rags, their heads cut off. The town was abuzz, though the women must have been tourists, since none of the locals was missing.

One night—not too late—Zhenya was walking home from a friend's house when, not far from home, she was suddenly grabbed from both sides. Her attackers were three teenagers, around sixteen or seventeen, and dark-skinned—that is, migrants from the South. Zhenya didn't know them, and they didn't know Zhenya; they'd have grown up while she was away at school. They gagged her and led her away, twisting her arms behind her back, as if they had done it before, and Zhenya hobbled along bent over, and was pushed and shoved, a knife pricking her back. They addressed each other in their tongue; Zhenya understood some of it—though they called themselves Greeks in the town, they were not Greeks. Zhenya could tell they were arguing about who should go first, since one of them supposedly had a bad disease. They yelled in the darkness of the night, arguing (partly in Russian), dragging

Zhenya with them, when suddenly everything became bright. It was as if someone had turned on a projector. The three man-boys stopped, momentarily letting go of Zhenya, and, seeing a construction site lit up before her, and an old man and a woman standing there among the broken rocks, she rushed toward them as fast as she could, taking the rag out of her mouth and yelling, "Kill me! Kill me!" She stopped beside the old man, reaching out her swollen arms to him and begging: "Kill me! Just don't let them have me!"

The three boys started arguing indignantly that she was a whore, that she owed them, they'd paid! They yelled this in Russian.

The old man dismissed them with a single wave of his hand, saying, in their language, "Leave." And the three turned around like soldiers and disappeared back into the night, having received an order in their own tongue.

The old man told Zhenya that he would walk her home. The woman stayed at the construction site; she held her head down, and Zhenya caught only a brief glimpse of her but was struck by her resemblance to her mother. Zhenya was afraid to leave, but the old man started off, and she had to follow. The old man brought her to a strange house. Zhenya couldn't see anything in the dark, and entering a room that looked like a cupboard, she heard the old man lock the door behind her and walk away. Zhenya sat down on the floor, felt with her hands for the rough, uneven wall, then leaned against it and fell asleep.

In the morning she awoke outside. She was sitting with her back against the rough trunk of a poplar tree in the middle of an overgrown empty lot. Zhenya began to run, not knowing in which direction, until finally she found the road back to town and her grandmother's and went to sleep in a little shack outside the house. It was early morning when she finally got home. She told her grandmother that she'd slept over at a friend's house since she was afraid to walk at night. Zhenya also said that she wanted to return to school right away.

Her grandmother probably understood everything—Zhenya's arms were badly swollen and covered with bruises, her face was puffy, and the corner of her mouth was torn.

The grandmother said she hadn't slept all night and had instead gone through the chest with all their old things and found her daughter's earrings and an icon. She wanted to give them to Zhenya.

Zhenya put on her mother's earrings, which were exactly the same as the ones she'd recently used for payment, gathered her few things, including the icon, and set off for the train station. She decided to go by the construction site on the way, so as to see the old man and the woman who looked like her mother. But there was nothing there: no construction site, no empty lot. It was a sunny day, and all around were houses and gardens.

Walking alongside her, her grandmother kept silent about the fact that they weren't heading toward the train station at all but rather in the opposite direction, toward the dump on the edge of town. Suddenly Zhenya said that she thought her mother's grave might be nearby, and that they should look for it under a poplar log in an empty lot. The grandmother objected that her daughter had disappeared in an entirely different town, but Zhenya didn't hear her. She simply kept looking for the log, and at the first one she found she sat down on the ground and burst into tears.

They both sat there like that for a long time, crying, and then Zhenya, in her winter dress with long sleeves, left that town for good. She no longer searched for her mother in mental hospitals and jails, though she kept wearing the earrings, and still does.

Two Kingdoms

IN THE BEGINNING THEY FLEW THROUGH A CELESTIAL PAR-
adise, through a glorious blue landscape and over thick curly
clouds. You could tell the stewardess was from the place they
were going to: she wore a wondrous linen suit with no but-
tons. The beverages she served had a foreign taste.

The passengers all dozed with fatigue. As Lina walked
through the rows she was struck by how much everyone
resembled everyone else, with their yellowish faces and
black crew cuts. She even became frightened, thinking an
army regiment was being transported with her to this new
place. All the soldiers slept, reclining in the same exact
way, their parched mouths half-open. But then again they
might have been the embassy staff of some exotic southern
country.

Then night fell. Lina had never flown so far and for so
long, and she spent part of the night in the bathroom, looking out the little window. She saw stars above and around, as
well as far below, where they could easily have been mistaken
for dim village lights. Racing along through the black night,

through the astral profusion, one's soul felt elated, aware of itself at the center of the universe, in absolute and utter darkness among the large, furry, flickering stars. Alone among the stars!

Lina even began to cry. It was with difficulty now that she recalled the moments of parting from her family and everything she loved: it all seemed so enormous and confusing, and she could no longer remember what happened first and what happened next. The miraculous reappearance of Vasya with the tickets and the marriage license; the complex bureaucratic formalities; her mother's tears when the women dressed Lina in white and wheeled her downstairs into the elevator, where Vasya took her in his arms and carried her to the car. Either she fainted or she was sick from the drive—everything was like a dream: the stupid music, the bewildered, terrified spectators on all sides, the mirrors showing Vasya with his beard, and then Lina, gray, emaciated, in white lace and with sunken eyes.

They must have done the operation they were planning before she left, but what happened after that, Lina was already unable to say. Her mother was howling for some reason, the sound muffled as if by a pillow, and her son was crying, frightened by the music, the flowers, and Lina's face. He was crying the way frightened children always cry when they see their mother being beaten or taken from them: he shrieked loudly; it was heart-wrenching. He was too small—he had to stay with his grandmother because Lina needed another operation, in a foreign city, a foreign country, and with this new husband, this Vasya who had appeared out of nowhere with his beard.

He was really just a rumor, this Vasya. He would show up once a year, emerge from the crowd, kiss her hand, taking it in his big cold palm, and promise Lina fantastic treasures and a future for her son—not now, but soon. Later. Just then, at that particular moment, it was impossible. But later, later he would take them away, her and her son, and her honorable mom, too, to an earthly paradise far far away, somewhere on the shores of a warm sea, amid marble columns, where they had—was it little elves?—flying about. In short, she'd live like Thumbelina from the fairy tale.

And later, when Lina became seriously ill at all of thirty-seven, this Vasya appeared more often, bringing consolation. He visited after the first operation, walked right into the intensive care unit—it was very touching—when Lina was about to reunite with her Maker, lying with an IV and staring at her scrawny, disappearing arm. He came clad in white, like a doctor (actually, he always adored white things); the only problem was he walked barefoot. But no one noticed him. He wanted to take Lina away immediately when he saw the state she was in, and her stitches. Just then the nurse came running in, out of breath, shooed Vasya away, and gave Lina another shot, then called for the doctor, and Vasya disappeared for a long time.

The next time, though, he came straight to the hospital, told her that everything had been arranged, that her mother had said yes, that she and the boy could be brought over later, and that he'd leave them everything they needed.

But Lina had to be taken there right away—there was no time to lose. In his country they knew how to cure Lina's illness. They had discovered a vaccine, and so on. By then Lina didn't care either way. She was so tired this second time, she couldn't resist anything—the sickness, death. They had her on very strong narcotics, and she was floating as through a fog.

She wasn't even tormented this time by thoughts of her boy, her little Seryozha.

"And if I die in this hospital?" Lina had thought. "Would that be any better? This way I'll live, and then I'll bring him over to me."

So Vasya arranged everything, although the doctors insisted on an operation, saying that without it the patient wouldn't make it through another day. Vasya waited for them to finish the operation, meanwhile took care of all the formalities, and came to pick up Lina and take her again directly from intensive care. They drove her carefully, changed her attire—for some reason, because of her new outfit, she could no longer see or hear anything—and when she awoke she was already flying through the blue sky and the endless, deserted, fluffy field of clouds. Lina was surprised to find herself sitting next to Vasya, and, what is more, drinking some light sparkling wine from a glass. Later she even got up—Vasya was asleep, exhausted from all the preparations—and walked around the plane with a surprisingly light step. Nothing hurt—they must have given her some painkillers.

The plane passed very low over a magnificent city that unfolded underneath them like an architectural model, with a glistening river, bridges, and an enormous toy cathedral. It looked so much like Paris!

And then right away came the roar of the plane landing, and the plane, with its flat nose as wide as a hotel window, rattling and shaking like a wheelbarrow, literally parked itself in a quiet garden. Lina's big window had a door in it, and in the distance the river sparkled with its bridges and also some kind of triumphal arch.

"Place de Pigalle!" Lina said for some reason and pointed. "Look!"

Vasya went to open the door, which led out to the terrace, and a fairy tale life began.

Lina wasn't allowed to go across the river just yet, though her treatment had started and was going well. Vasya would leave and then be gone all day. He never forbade Lina anything, but it was clear that the river and the cathedral were still very far off. In the meantime she began to go out little by little, wandering down the same tiny street, since she still wasn't very strong.

Everyone here, she noticed, looked just like Vasya, like the hippies she'd seen in foreign films. Long hair, lovely thin arms, white clothes, beards for the men, even little wreaths. The stores, it was true, had everything you could imagine, but, first of all, Vasya never left Lina any money—it must have all gone to pay for her treatment, which was probably very expensive.

And second, it was impossible to send packages from here, or even letters. People in this country just didn't write! There wasn't a single sheet of paper anywhere, not a single pen. There was no connection—perhaps Lina had found herself in a kind of quarantine, a transitional place.

Across the river she saw the bubbling, real life of a foreign city.

They had everything here, too—restaurants, stores. But there was no connection. For now Lina moved by holding onto the wall with both hands, like an infant who has just learned to walk. When she complained to Vasya that she wanted to go shopping, he immediately brought her a pile of clothing, including some that had been worn—men's, women's, children's, and what's more of different sizes. He also brought a suitcase full of shoes, the way friends from abroad used to bring them to Russia. Among the clothing was a pair of gray men's army-issue long underwear, which Lina found a little embarrassing. Who knew what those were, or whose! And what was she supposed to do with all this clothing? She had quickly begun to wear only Vasya's things—a white chemise, and over that a thin white linen dress. She and Vasya were the same height, and Vasya's build, though he was healthy, turned out to be the same as that of the emaciated Lina. She cried over the mountain of clothes, and in the evening told Vasya that she really wanted to send a package to her mother and little Seryozha, and pointed at the two small piles. Vasya frowned and didn't say anything; the next morning all the clothes were gone.

Vasya worked, it turned out, on this side of the river, in this zone, and he didn't have any desire to go across the river to the arches and cathedrals. Lina was forced to get used to his quiet, measured existence. She knew, of course, from her old life, that anything could happen: the youthful Vasya could fall in love with another woman and leave her. He didn't really love her, this Vasya with his beard, though he protected her from all cares. Their food appeared all by itself, their clothes sparkled.

When did he find the time? Their room, which Lina in her feverish state still imagined to be part of a plane or a spacecraft, looked out on a white-columned terrace, but there was no joy there. Lina was brave, enduring her separation from little Seryozha, her mother, her girlfriends, and her college friend Lev. She understood now that her condition was incurable, and the best she could hope for was to keep to her current state—without pain, but also without strength. What talk could there be of bringing her loud little Seryozha here, with his wild tears and eyes all red from crying! And then her mother especially, with her insinuating hellos, and also tearful. There was no grief here and no tears. It was another country.

Annoyed, Lina watched the people who lived here hovering in their circle dance over the river to the monotonous music of the harps (a silly activity, by the way). She observed their silent sessions at the long common tables in the restaurant, before glasses of the lovely local wine.

Lina very much wanted to tell her girlfriends back home and her mom what she thought of all this, to at least drop them a line to say that everything was all right, that her treatment was going well, that the stores have everything but you can't buy it—first of all because it's very expensive, and second because no one dresses that way here—that the food is strange but she can't eat too much yet anyway. And so on. That she wants to send Seryozha a package but so far no one is going back there, and there seems to be no postal service between their two countries. Lina dragged herself down the streets, holding onto whatever she could, and wrote letters home in her head.

Eventually, though, Lina began to see that there would be no letters. Vasya definitively promised that her mom and Seryozha would visit eventually, especially her mom. But her mom without Seryozha? Or Seryozha without his grandmother? "In time," said the bearded Vasya. "In time."

Lina wanted to start buying things in preparation for her mother's visit, but Vasya made it clear that by then everything would be taken care of.

In fact, no one here worried about the future—everyone was too busy—but nonetheless things were organized perfectly, comfortably, cleanly. Vasya worked at a bookstore that he'd inherited from an aunt, but never brought home any books since Lina could not read the language, and the store had nothing in Russian. It turned out Vasya could not even write in Russian.

Then the time finally came when Lina learned to move in the flying way of the natives. It turned out to be very simple. You just got up on a step above the ground and then took a big wide stride into the air. The next stride, too, came from the force of the initial push, and every stride thereafter was freer and lighter, as in a dream. Bearded Vasya didn't say anything, but at the appointed time he disappeared forever, probably across the river into the wealthy city. Lina was left on her own, although fully provided for. At first she thought, without fear or tears, that soon they would chase her out of their spacecraft—the food couldn't always be in the refrigerator! But the refrigerator kept filling up, as if through a dumbwaiter, though Lina didn't eat anything, just drank juice and stayed healthy.

And then the day finally came when, after much lonely and sad contemplation, she tore herself from her front steps and with wide strides raced to the bank of the river to the circle dance and, stepping between two dancers, who momentarily separated their hands, entered the stream and began to fly around the circle. She understood, she knew, that something was wrong, and she no longer wanted to have her mother here, or her son. She didn't even want to run into that army regiment again, and in fact she didn't want to see anyone again, or if she did see someone she didn't want to know who it was, hoped she'd be unable to distinguish between the young, pale, calm faces in the circle dance, flying free like her—and hoping not to meet anyone at all anymore, in this kingdom of the dead, and hoping never to learn just how much they grieved in that other kingdom, of the living.

There's Someone in the House

THERE IS CLEARLY SOMEONE IN THE HOUSE. WALK INTO THE bedroom: something falls in the living room. Look for the cat: it's sitting on the little table in the front hall, its ears pricked up; it clearly heard something, too. Walk into the living room: a scrap of paper has fallen, all by itself, from the piano, with someone's phone number on it, you can't tell whose. It just flew off the piano soundlessly and lies on the carpet, white and alone.

Someone isn't being careful, thinks the woman who lives here. Someone isn't even trying to hide anymore.

A person can be afraid of rodents, insects, little ants in the bath, even a lonely cockroach that's stumbled into your apartment in a drugged state, fleeing the disinfection campaign at the neighbors'—which is to say, he's just standing naked and defenseless, in plain view. But a person can be afraid of anything when she's alone with her cat and everyone has departed, all her old family, leaving this little human roach completely by herself, unprotected.

On weekends, especially, it appears that things are falling

and Someone is secretly, soundlessly creeping from room to room. That's how it seems.

The woman doesn't tell anyone about her poltergeist: It's still hiding, not knocking, not causing mischief, not setting anything on fire. The refrigerator isn't hopping around the apartment; the poltergeist isn't chasing her into a corner. Really there's nothing to complain about.

But Something has definitely moved in, some kind of living emptiness, small of stature but energetic and pushy, sneaking and slithering along the floor—that's how it seems. No wonder the cat's ears pricked up.

"Come now," the woman says to her cat. It's a strange and quiet cat, as all cats are. It won't let itself be petted, won't lie on its mistress's knee when beckoned, but will suddenly jump up by itself at an inopportune time. "What are you afraid of, little one?" says the woman cheerfully. "Calm down; there's nothing there."

The cat twists away and leaves the room.

The woman watches television until she falls asleep. She watches intently, her face pressed to the screen. She immerses herself in its bluish rays, floats off to foreign worlds, becomes frightened, intrigued, heartbroken—in short, she *lives*. This is her place, on the couch. And then—*crash*! Something just fell in the bedroom.

This time there was an awful racket. It really collapsed, whatever it was. The sound is still echoing through the apartment.

The woman runs into the room and stands there in shock. The shelf with all her records has collapsed. They've scattered all over, spread out in a fanlike formation on the unmade sofa bed and on the floor. If someone—you get three guesses who—had been sleeping there, she'd have gotten the sharp corner of the shelf right in the skull. But it didn't happen. Now the wall features two gaping wounds: the nails, driven into the wall by someone we'd rather not bring to mind right now, have fallen out. Of course they weren't nails exactly—they have some other name. It was a major production at the time, she remembers. It could almost have passed for love. He'd had to use a drill.

But these nails, or not-nails, whatever, had in the end been inserted, and in the end they'd given way.

The shelf now lies on the piano—that's why it made such a terrible racket, with echoes like in the mountains.

The piano—that, too, was an adventure. A little girl tried to learn to play it. Her mother insisted, forced her to sit there and practice. Nothing came of it; stubbornness won out in the end, the stubbornness that protects us from the will of others, that defends our right to live our life the way we want. Even if it means life will turn out worse than anyone planned, will turn into a poor life—but it'll be one's own, however it is, even without music, even without talent. Without concerts for the family, maybe—but also without needless worries that someone else plays the piano better. The mother always worried that other children were more talented than her daughter. The daughter heard this enough times and had her revenge by becoming a total nonentity, a fact that both mother and daughter freely acknowledged.

Then it all dissolved, all those family dramas straight out of Turgenev; now all that remained was the piano and the old records that crashed into it. The mother had collected classical music, once. The mother had spent hours discussing her daughter over the phone, spilling her child's secrets as if they didn't cost a thing. Now there was no mother, no daughter, no shelf for the records. Just a woman standing in a doorway, awestruck by the scene of destruction that was her bedroom. There could be no more sleeping on that bed—everything was ruined, soaked through with dust. She had to change the sheets. She had to wash, clean, find a new place for everything—but where? There was no room.

The woman retreats to the living room, closing the door to the bedroom as if for the last time.

If she could just catch the Creature by its ugly invisible tail. But then what? She'd just die of fright and disgust. You couldn't kill It, after all. You couldn't crush It with your heel. So there wasn't any point to catching It, really.

It clearly wants something, this Creature, It's trying to get at something. Like the mother was trying to get at something with her daughter. Now if she could just figure out what It wants, she could—she's done this before—defeat Its design. She could seize the initiative. That's a classic maneuver—meet your enemy halfway. Like when they light a fire to battle another fire in the forest—if they intersect in the right spot, they'll both go out for lack of oxygen.

Once upon a time, for example, the mother had owned an expensive set of German china, an investment for a rainy day, and she guarded this china with her life in case they'd have to sell it to pay for a funeral (hers)—and one time, when, in a fit, the daughter had hurled one of the cups to the floor, the mother cold-bloodedly began smashing the rest of the set ("*slut!*" went the noise it made, "*slut!*"), piece by piece by piece, nearly driving her daughter insane, and declaring, to top it off, "I'm going to die, all right, but you'll be left with nothing."

Yet here's the question: Does the Creature want her total annihilation, or just to drive her into the street?

Well, she can't leave the house. There's nowhere to go. And maybe a certain someone will want to come back (thinks the mother-daughter). So she has to stay. If It's wreaking havoc, she'll have to fight It. The way Kutuzov fought Napoleon—by making his position *uncomfortable*. This is very wise, thinks the woman. The Creature will be defeated.

✝

The decision came painfully at first, but then it grew easier. She went into the kitchen and smashed all the plates and cups. She flung the fragments through the apartment. With great difficulty, but triumphantly at last, she pulled down the kitchen cabinet and let it drop on top of the broken dishes. Having done this she noticed that the cabinet had in fact been hanging just barely on its screws. One section simply fell off the wall when she pulled it down, like a fish leaving a pond—which is to say easily, very easily. And the cabinet itself, it turned out, was falling apart, the back panel having come undone in the corner. So in fact this cabinet had been poised to fall and destroy all the dishes anyway! Not to mention anyone who happened to be standing underneath it at the time.

Now the mother-daughter gained courage. What intuition she'd had, it turned out! She'd made this first step in her defense and immediately uncovered a plot! It was a battle of wills, clearly—and it had been joined!

She spent the night on the couch in the living room, then lay in wait for a day, plotting.

Her patience was rewarded: There came a noise from the bedroom, now covered in dust, the records fanned out across it, the echoes from yesterday still hanging in the air. In she went. A plot was clearly underfoot. Her ancient sofa bed stood there, unfolded. In the mornings she used to remove the bedding and place it under the sofa, then fold the whole thing, but at some point she'd stopped—after all, what was the point? Now the m-d (mother-daughter) grabs a hammer and lifts the mattress, sliding the records all to one side. Then she starts pulling out every screw from the frame. She is bent over under the dusty mattress, working frantically in the darkness. And once again it turns out she was right! The screws come out so easily; clearly they were on their way out already. Another day or two and the whole thing would have collapsed on its own. Once again she's anticipated a terrorist attack. Once again she's outwitted It.

Now the fold-out sofa won't fold at all—so be it. Covered with debris, with dust, with a pile of records and her crumpled-up sheets, that's just how it will remain forever, like a sacred funeral ground that you must give a kilometer's berth to. Like the memorial to a terrible earthquake.

And now she must stay ahead, refuse whatever comes easily, seek new avenues, find what is still whole and unbroken.

With one blow of the hammer she smashes the television set. The noise is moderate. It was an old television, but it still showed all the programs, though now only in black and white.

She couldn't have thought of a better plan. If It had wanted to strike a truly terrible blow, It would have blown up the television first. She could well imagine the results: her face cut by glass shards (she always placed herself right in front of the screen when she watched) and her apartment on fire. Everything burned. Including of course you-know-who, carried from the apartment in a body bag. It was the sort of thing they regularly showed on that very television.

And it is the most painful blow because television was everything to the m-d. It was her support, her joy, the center of her little household. It was to the television that she hurried when she returned home from grocery shopping. It was for the sake of the television that she'd pick up the free advertising supplements containing the TV guide. Nor would she throw them away afterward, but would pore over them sometimes, remembering.

Still the roof over her head is more valuable than television.

So as not to dwell on this painful dilemma (i.e. , to be or not to be), the m-d takes all her clothes out of the wardrobe and shoves them into a big potato sack she finds under the pile of old rags in the cupboard. She's been meaning to throw away *that* pile forever, but now it'll have to wait—it is filled with worn-out jackets and skirts and rubber boots, all in case she decides to take a trip to the countryside, or, alternatively, if a war (or famine) breaks out and she has to evacuate. She also keeps her old curtains and blankets in there, including children's blankets, in case the heat is shut off during the winter the way it was during the Siege. The cupboard is a monument to generations of poverty, whereas the wardrobe contains her current life. And so it is the clothes from the wardrobe that go straight into the potato sack.

It is dark already, on this second day of her counteroffensive, and she drags her sack of clothing-potatoes to the open window and pushes it out into the empty space beyond. In the sack are her blouses, dresses, a jacket, her winter coat. Her underwear, scarves, gloves, hats, berets, belts, kerchiefs. A good pair of winter hose. Pants. Three sweaters. Two full skirts and one midi-length skirt. And then her sheets—clean sheets, smelling of freshness and soap. All her towels. Her pillowcases and sheets, and duvets, one with embroidery. Oh, God. But at least they hadn't been lost in the fire.

In the wake of her potato sack she launches a painting in a gold frame and three chairs, one after the other.

From down below she hears someone yelling, some curses, a hollow male cry.

She quickly closes the window. Phew.

There is nothing to wear now, just her bathrobe over her nightshirt and her last pair of underwear.

She lies down on the cot, on top of the old TV guides. The blanket and pillows remain in the bedroom, victims of the earthquake. She covers herself up with a fresh advertising supplement and goes to sleep.

In the morning, after a good night's sleep, the m-d looks around and thinks that now she really fears nothing, absolutely nothing, and that now in fact she isn't even afraid to abandon her current life, her household, the roof above her head.

She begins a gradual retreat from the apartment. Carefully the m-d steps through the doorway, leaving her keys in a purse on the table. But first she has to let her cat out.

She thinks about this for a while. Theoretically she could leave the cat inside the apartment, but the cat isn't a strategically valuable object (supposedly) and isn't worth sending into the Creature's maw. That is, the sacrifice of a living thing was never part of her battle plan. The m-d wishes to be harder on herself than on her cat. The question is, whom will it be worse for, her or her cat, when m-d begins her new life, without anything, but still somehow hearing the fading sounds of the meowing, straining, locked-in Lulu. The m-d begins debating herself—it would still be worse for the cat, she decides. Who was Lulka that someone should take the trouble to starve her to death? Just an accidental animal, taken down, once, from a tree.

Trying not to think about it too hard, the m-d decides to kick the cat out of the apartment. But here an interesting thing happens. The m-d is prepared for life on the outside—but the cat is not. When the m-d picks her up and drapes her over her elbow, determined to carry her out with her, the cat begins to shake with tiny tremors, like a boiling kettle. Like the suburban train right before it sets off. Like a very sick child in the grip of fever. The cat is shaking—fearing, it seems, for its life.

"What is it?" the m-d asks soothingly. "What are we afraid of? Come on, kitty. You were always trying to run out. So run. Run for your life!"

It's true—the cat was always rushing out to the stairs, or guarding the door, driving everyone crazy with her hoarse moans. She cried at night. But it was dangerous to let her out—what if she never returned? After all, the m-d loved animals. Even if, just now, she doesn't.

Joyful, alive, she drops the cat to the floor on the landing outside the apartment and then slams the door behind them both—there!

In a robe and slippers, she stands at the precipice of her new fate. She is her own master: she's defeated the Creature. It can romp and slither around all it wants, if it intends to follow her, in these huge wide-open spaces of the great outdoors.

The cat sits on its tail as if it's been kicked. It huddles down pitifully and looks somehow . . . pensive. The woman descends half a flight of stairs and turns around: The cat sits frozen still and staring straight ahead, its eyes filmed over as if with cataracts, its pupils like little black seeds drowning

in the green lakes that are its eyes. Its little face looks bony.
Its skull suddenly emerges, it seems, and you can see its out-
line under the cat's black fur. Death itself is on that stairwell,
dressed up in a thin fur coat.

The woman nearly bursts into tears! The cat is preparing
to die. The street awaits it, and wild dogs, and hunger. The cat
can't fight for its life—it doesn't know how. Tonight they will
kick her out of the entryway, plant a boot in her stomach as
soon as she takes her first pee.

The m-d pauses on her triumphant march downstairs.
She imagines the cat falling apart the way everything else
has—the dishes, the chairs, the television, her clothes.

The Creature will celebrate a total victory.

"That's a little much," the m-d thinks to herself. "To give up
everything to such a nothing. I think we'll make it, after all."

Lulu sits there like the scarecrow of a cat, her glassy,
cloudy eyes popping out of her head. Her tail, usually so energetic, subtly expressing all her thoughts, now lies like a dusty
dead little rope. All her fur is dusty, drab, and sick.

The woman immediately takes the kitty up in her arms,
presses its stone-cold body to her own, rings the neighbor's
doorbell, quickly calls the super, and sits down on the chair
she is offered to wait for someone to come up and force open
the door.

†

She walks into her ruined apartment, sets Lulu down on the
floor, and looks around her with the eyes of a new owner. It is
as if everything were new, strange, and interesting.

There are still shoes in the hallway! In the kitchen, all her pots and pans have survived, as has a salad bowl and a coffee mug. Her forks and spoons! "What luxury," thinks the woman, who's been ready to graze downstairs, outside, near the trash containers, looking for a discarded can she could use for drinking water, and a moldy piece of bread to eat.

"Would I ever find this kind of luxury in the trash?" murmurs the woman as she opens the refrigerator and sees a saucer and a soup bowl, with the boiled (!) fruits of the earth, with beets and potatoes. And a little plate of fish for Lulka!

This apartment has everything. It is warm, and outside of the kitchen it is relatively clean; the water runs in the bath, there is soap, a telephone! And her bed! There is still a sheet and a duvet, luckily. There are lots of records on the couch and a record player in the corner, forgotten there; someone in this house used to like to listen to music—either the mother or the daughter, she can't remember which.

The mother-daughter quickly cleans the shattered dishes in the kitchen—and so what: it isn't the first time this has happened in this particular house. She makes a series of trips to the trash container outside; on the third trip, as she spills her shards into the container, two men in soiled, dirty clothing and sacks over their shoulders approach carefully, wait until she moves away, and immediately dive into the trash. They behave like shades of men—shy, unnoticeable, dark.

The m-d takes a look at the ground beneath her window. Naturally the contents of her potato sack have been picked off long ago. Well, someone else would have to walk around in her sweater and pants, while she, liberated, would walk around in nothing. That's right. Returning to her clean, swept, washed apartment, m-d is surprised first of all by how timid she'd been—she failed to throw away her groceries, failed to smash the insides of the refrigerator, and kept all the lamps and bulbs intact.

Suddenly she remembers, and puts out the plate of fish for her Lulka.

But Lulka just sits there like a post, frozen in the middle of the front hall, and her eyes still look like grapes cleared of their skin, with a barely visible pit inside.

The breath of death must have frozen her frightened soul.

The woman doesn't try to console her cat—her task now is to put everything in order as quickly as possible, and then the cat will also be all right.

And, as often happens when one member of a family is momentarily indecisive, afraid, or hysterical, the other takes heart and saves the situation. The woman begins moving faster—quickly placing the shelf atop the piano, gathering the records, removing the blanket and quickly washing it in the bath.

It turns out there are still some towels left—a little one on a hook in the kitchen and two drying on a radiator in the bath.

"It's all right," the woman tells Lulu. "We'll make it."

Not only that, she immediately finds a screwdriver and gathers the screws from the fold-out sofa and screws them back in tight, then folds it into its daytime position.

There!

It had been so easy to destroy everything, and it is so hard to fix, clean, and order it again. She has to bend, crawl into corners, gather shards, carry out trash, drive the screws back in! The television is the worst. She has to wait for dark and then throw it out the window with all her might, then pick it up downstairs—the woman lives in a walk-up—and carry the remains to the trash in her little grocery cart.

It is as if a war had ravaged the territory of the m-d's peaceful apartment—a veritable war.

The living room looks empty without the television and the chairs.

But a person can make do without all sorts of things, so long as she's still alive. There is nothing to watch, true, but all of a sudden in the darkness you could make out a shelf of the m-d's favorite books. She puts on her once-favorite record—the tango!

Then, as the music plays, she begins to go through the backpacks and suitcases filled with her old clothes. Her whole life unspools before her, like a newsreel. The beloved apparitions rise up before her and around her, though none of the old things quite fit the m-d anymore—she must have grown fat sitting in front of the TV all day. All right. She has a few pieces of fabric, and there is a sewing machine in the corner of the closet, and she could probably put together a reasonable skirt to go with the several blouses that still more or less close on her.

And anyway for many years the m-d has worn only her old and ragged things, keeping her clean and nearly brand-new clothing for special occasions—which never arrived.

As she is working this out for herself, the m-d also gathers a big bag of old clothes and shoes, recalling the shades of men who'd greeted her last trash trip with such enthusiasm.

God, what a life now opens before the m-d! But the cat still sits in shock in the hallway, like someone who's lived through too much, and stares ahead at the same spot with murky, unseeing eyes.

Then suddenly the cat pricks up her ears.

The woman laughs.

Obviously the building is settling, drying, aging, boards are cracking—that's first of all. Moreover in all these apartments above, below, and to the sides, people are living, living people, and some of them are moving, something is breaking or being fixed, something is falling or cooking. "That's life!" says the woman loudly, addressing herself, as always, to the cat.

As for Lulu, she stands up lightly and heads for the kitchen, raising her front paws slowly, like a heavy tigress, which is strange given her emaciated state. Then she deliberately sits herself at her place, her nose to the corner, leans over, and takes a piece of fish into her mouth, nodding her head. She's decided to live.

Fairy Tales

Fairy Tale

The Father

THERE ONCE LIVED A FATHER WHO COULDN'T FIND HIS CHILdren. He went everywhere, asked everyone—had his little children come running in here? But whenever people responded with the simplest of questions—"What do they look like?" "What are their names?" "Are they boys or girls?"—he didn't know how to answer. He simply knew that his children were somewhere, and he kept looking. One time, late in the evening, he helped an old lady carry her bags to her apartment. The old lady didn't invite him in. She didn't even say thank you. Instead she suddenly told him to take the local train to the Fortieth Kilometer stop.

"What for?" he asked.

"What do you mean, what for?" And the old lady carefully closed the door behind her, bolting it and fastening the chain. Yet on his very first day off—and it was the middle of a cold, northern winter—he went off to the Fortieth Kilometer. For some reason the train kept stopping, for long stretches of time, and it was beginning to grow dark when they finally reached the station.

The hapless traveler found himself on the edge of a forest; for some reason he started tramping through snowdrifts until he reached its very heart. Soon he was on a well-beaten path, which in the twilight brought him to a little hut. He knocked on the door, but no one answered. He stepped into the hall, knocked again, and again there was nothing. Then he quietly entered the warm hut, took off his boots, coat, and hat, and began to look around. It was warm and clean inside, and a kerosene lamp was burning. Whoever lived there had just gone out, leaving their tea mug and kettle and bread, butter, and sugar on the table. The stove was warm. Our traveler was cold and hungry, and so, apologizing to anyone who might hear, he poured himself a cup of hot water. Then, after some thought, he ate a piece of bread and placed some money on the table. Meanwhile, outside it had grown completely dark, and the traveling father began to wonder what he should do. He didn't know the schedule of the trains, and he was in danger of finding himself in a snowbank, especially as the snow had been coming down hard and covering all the paths. The father collapsed on the bench and fell asleep. He was roused by a knock at the door. Raising himself from the bench he said, "Yes—come in."

A little child wrapped in some kind of frayed rag entered the hut.

He stopped at the table and froze, uncertain what to do.

"Now what's this?" said the future father, who wasn't yet fully awake. "Where are you coming from? How did you get here? Do you live here?"

The child shrugged and said "No."

"Who brought you here?"

The child shook his head, wrapped in his torn-up shawl.

"Are you by yourself?"

"Yes," said the boy.

"And your mom? Your dad?"

The boy sniffled and shrugged his shoulders.

"How old are you?"

"I don't know."

"All right. What's your name?"

The boy shrugged once again. His nose suddenly thawed and began to drip. He wiped it on his sleeve.

"Hold on there!" said the future dad. "That's why we have handkerchiefs." He wiped the boy's nose with a handkerchief and then started carefully taking off the boy's things. He unwound the shawl and took off the old fur hat and then the little overcoat, which was warm but very shabby.

"I'm a boy," the child said suddenly.

"Well, that's something already," said the man. He washed the boy's hands under the faucet—they were very small, with tiny fingernails. In fact the boy looked a lot like an old man, and at other moments, with his face scrunched up, his eyes and nose puffy, like he was wearing a space helmet. The man gave the boy some sweet tea and began feeding him bread.

It turned out the boy didn't know how to drink—the man had to give him the tea with a spoon. The man even began sweating, it was such hard work.

"All right, let's put you to bed," said the man, by now completely exhausted. "It's warmer on the stove, but you'd fall off. Sleep tight, sleep tight, till the morning comes all bright. We'll put you on the trunk and surround you with some chairs. Now as for sheets . . ."

The man searched the hut for a warm blanket but couldn't find one, and instead put down his warm coat for the child to lie on. He took off his sweater to cover the child with it. And then he looked at the trunk: What if there were something in there, some kind of blanket? The man opened the trunk and removed a blue silk quilted blanket, a pillow with lace, a little mattress, and a pile of little sheets. Under those he found a bundle of thin little shirts, also with lace, and then some warm flannel shirts and a knot of little knit pants, tied together with a light blue ribbon.

"How do you like that? There's a whole dowry here!" cried the man.

"Of course this belongs to another little boy—but all children get equally cold and equally hungry, so they should share with one another!" the future father concluded aloud. "It wouldn't be right for one child to have nothing, to walk around in rags, while another child has too much. Right?"

But the child had already fallen asleep on the bench.

With his clumsy hands the man prepared a luxurious blue bed, very carefully changed the child out of his old clothes and into clean ones, and put him down to sleep. For himself he threw his jacket on the floor next to the trunk and its chairs and covered himself with a sweater. The future father was so tired he fell asleep right away, and slept as he'd never slept before.

A knock on the door roused him.

A woman, all encrusted with snow but barefoot, entered the hut.

Leaping up and shielding the trunk, the man said: "I'm sorry, we made ourselves a little at home here. But I'll pay you."

"Excuse me," said the woman, not hearing him, "I got lost in the forest. I thought I'd come in here for a minute and warm up. It's a real blizzard out there; I thought I'd freeze to death. May I?"

The man realized that this woman didn't live here, either.

"I'll make you some tea," he said. "Please, sit down."

He had to feed firewood to the stove and look for the water bucket in the hall. Along the way he discovered a clay pot with potatoes that were still warm and another one with millet kasha and milk. "All right, we'll eat this," said the man. "But the kasha we'll save for the child."

"What child?" said the woman.

"Why, that one," said the man, and pointed to the trunk, where the baby slept sweetly, his little arms up over his head.

The woman knelt before the trunk and suddenly began to weep.

"Oh God, it's him, my little one!" she said.

And she kissed the edge of the blue blanket.

"Yours?" said the man, surprised. "What's his name?"

"I don't know—I haven't named him yet," said the woman. "I'm so tired after this night, a whole night of suffering. There was no one to help me. Not a soul in the world."

"What is he, then," said the man suspiciously, "a boy or a girl?"

"It doesn't matter—whatever he is, we'll love him."

And once again she kissed the edge of the blanket.

The man looked closely at the woman and saw that her face really did show traces of suffering—her lips were cracked, her eyes were hollow, her hair hung like string. Her legs turned out to be very thin. But some time passed, and the woman warmed up, apparently, and became prettier. Her eyes began to shine, and her sunken cheeks became rosy. She looked thoughtfully at the ugly, bald little boy. Her arms, holding tightly to the edge of the trunk, trembled.

The boy, too, changed. He shrank, and now looked like a little old man with a puffy nose and little eyes like slits.

This all struck the man as very strange—the way the woman and boy changed before his very eyes, literally in an instant. The man even grew frightened.

"Well, if he's yours, I won't bother you anymore," the failed father said, turning away. "I'll go. My train is leaving soon."

He dressed hurriedly and went away.

$$\dagger$$

It was already growing light out, and the path, strangely, was clear and well-beaten, as if there had been no blizzard the night before. Our traveler went away from the house quickly and after several hours of walking found himself at a house exactly like the one he'd left. No longer surprised, he went in without even knocking.

The hall was the same, the room was exactly the same, and just as before there was a teapot on the table and some bread. The traveler was tired and cold, and so without pausing he gulped down the tea, scarfed down a piece of bread, and lay down on the bench and waited. But no one came. Then the man leapt up and threw himself at the trunk. Once again there were kids' clothes inside, though this time they were warm little clothes—a little coat and hat, tiny little felt boots, warm little flannel pants, even a resplendent snowsuit, and at the bottom of the trunk a little fur sleeping bag with a hood. The man immediately thought that the boy must have nothing to wear outside—sure, he had some shirts, and all sorts of junk, but that was it! Apologizing to the empty room, he took only the most necessary items—the fur sleeping bag, snowsuit, boots, and hat. Then he also grabbed the sled, which stood in the corner, because he noticed there was another one in the other corner.

Once again begging forgiveness, he took from the pile of felt boots behind the trunk one adult pair that looked like they would fit a woman—she had been barefoot! With this load he ran as fast as he could through the cold back to the first hut. Already there was no one there. The teapot was still hot, and there was bread on the table. The trunk was empty.

"She must have dressed him in silk and lace," said the failed father. "But that's so silly—I have everything he needs!"

He ran out the door onto the other path and, dragging the sled behind him, soon caught up with the woman, who could barely stand and even swayed a little. Her bare feet were red from the snow. She carried the child wrapped in all his silky things.

"Hold on!" cried the father. "Wait! This won't do at all! First you need to dress a fellow up. I have everything he needs."

He took the child from her, and she, obediently, closing her eyes, gave him her burden, and together they walked back to their hut. Only then did the father remember the strange old lady whose bags he had carried home, and he asked the woman: "Tell me, did the old woman give you the address, too?"

"No," said the woman, who was nearly asleep on her feet, "she only told me the name of the train station, Fortieth Kilometer."

But just then the child started crying, and both of them rushed to change his clothes, and he was suddenly so small that no boots could fit him, and instead they had to put him in diapers, wrap him up in a blanket, and that's when the fur sleeping bag with its hood came in handy. The rest of it they tied up in a bundle. The woman put on her new boots, and the three of them continued back together. The newfound father carried the baby, and the woman dragged the things, and along the way they forgot all about how they met, and the name of the station. They remembered only that there had been a trying night, a long road, and painful loneliness—but now they'd given birth to a child and found what they'd been looking for.

The Cabbage-patch Mother

THERE ONCE LIVED A WOMAN WHO HAD A TINY LITTLE DAUghter named Droplet. The girl was just a tiny droplet of a baby, and she never grew. Her mother took her to doctors, but as soon as she showed her to them, they refused to treat her! No, they said—and that was that. They didn't even ask any questions about her.

So then the mother decided to play a trick: she wouldn't show her little Droplet to the next doctor. She went to his office, sat down, and asked: "What should you do if your child isn't growing properly?"

To which the doctor replied, as a doctor should: "What's wrong with the child? What's the child's medical history? What is the child's diet?" And so on.

"This child wasn't born," the poor mother explained. "I found her in a head of cabbage, young cabbage. I took off the top leaf, and there she was, a little cabbage-patch girl, a little dewdrop, this big"—she showed him with her fingers—"a little droplet. I took her with me, and I've been raising her ever since, but she hasn't grown at all, and it's been two years."

"Show me the child," said the doctor.

The girl's mother took out a matchbox she kept in her breast pocket, and out of this matchbox she took half of a hollowed bean, and in that cradle, wiping the sleep from her eyes with her tiny little fists, sat a tiny little girl.

The mother took a magnifying glass from her purse, and with this magnifying glass the doctor began examining the child.

"A splendid girl," the doctor said under his breath. "In good health, well nourished—you've done an excellent job, mother. Now get on your feet, little girl. That's right. Good."

The little droplet climbed out of her little bean and walked around on the doctor's desk, back and forth.

"Well," the doctor said. "I'll tell you this: She's a splendid girl, but this isn't the right place for her to live. Now where exactly she *should* be living, I can't tell, but definitely not here with us. We're not the right crowd for her. This isn't the right place."

The mother said: "It's true. She tells me she has dreams about her life on a distant star. She says everyone there had little wings, and they flew through the fields—she did, too— and she ate pollen and dew from wild flowers, and they had an elder, who was preparing them, because some of them would have to leave, and they all waited in terror for the day their wings would melt—because then their leader would take them to the top of a high mountain, where there was an opening to a cave, and steps leading down to it, and the ones whose wings had melted would descend into the cave, and everyone else watched them as they went down, farther and farther down until they were as small as little droplets."

Sitting on the desk, the girl nodded.

"And then my little princess also had to leave, and she cried and walked down the steps, and that's where her dream ends, and she wakes up on my kitchen table, in a cabbage leaf."

"Interesting," said the doctor. "And, tell me, what about you? What's happened in your life? What's your medical history?"

"Me?" said the woman. "What's it matter? I love my girl more than I love my life. It's so terrible to think she's going to return to the place she came from . . . As for my history, well, my husband left me when I was pregnant, and I didn't have the baby . . . I went to a doctor who referred me to a hospital, and there they killed my baby inside me. Now I pray for him. Maybe he's in that place, in the land of dreams?"

"Interesting," said the doctor. "I see now. I'm going to write you a note, and you'll take it to a certain person. He's a hermit, and he lives in the forest. He's a very strange man, and sometimes it's impossible to find him, but he might help you. Who knows."

The woman put her little girl back into the cradle made out of a little bean, put the bean back into the matchbox, put the matchbox back into her pocket, and took her magnifying glass and left—directly for the forest, to look for the hermit there.

She found him sitting on a pile of garbage near the road. Without uttering a word she showed him the doctor's note and then pointed at her breast pocket.

"You need to put her back where you found her," the hermit said, "and not look at her anymore."

"Back where? The produce store?"

"Stupid woman! Where'd they find her?"

"In a cabbage patch. But I don't know where that is."

"Stupid woman!" the hermit yelled. "You knew how to sin; you must know how to save yourself."

"Where's the cabbage patch?" the mother asked again.

"Enough," said the hermit. "And don't look at her."

The woman cried, bowed down, crossed herself, kissed the hermit's smelly, frayed sweatshirt, and walked away. When she turned around a minute later, there was no longer any hermit, or any trash pile—just a wisp of fog.

The woman grew scared and ran. Evening was approaching, and she kept on running through empty fields. Suddenly she saw a patch filled with rows of little cabbage buds poking through the earth.

It was growing dark out, and the woman stood there in the drizzle, holding her breast pocket, thinking she couldn't leave her daughter here in the cold and the fog. The girl would get scared and start crying!

So with her bare hands the woman dug up a big clump of soil and a cabbage bud with it, wrapped this into her slip, and dragged the heavy bundle with her to the city and all the way home.

As soon as she crossed the doorstep, falling down with exhaustion, she took out her largest pot and placed the clump of soil and the cabbage into the pot and then put all this on her windowsill. And to avoid ever looking at it, she closed the curtain.

But then she thought: she'd have to water the little cabbage. And in order to water the cabbage, she'd have to look at it.

So she took her pot out onto the balcony, into real field conditions. If there was rain, there'd be rain, and if there was wind, there'd be wind, and birds, and so on. If the baby lived and grew inside her, like all other babies, then she'd be protected from the cold and the wind, but her little Droplet was different—she couldn't hide inside her mother's body; she'd have only one cabbage leaf to protect her.

Carefully moving aside the young, firm leaves of the cabbage bud, the mother put her little daughter inside it. Her Droplet didn't even wake up—in general she loved sleeping and was an unusually quiet, happy, and easygoing child. The cabbage leaves were hard, naked, and cold, and they immediately closed around little Droplet.

The mother quietly stepped back from the balcony, closed the door, and began living all by her lonesome again, just as before. She went to work, returned from work, prepared herself some food, and never looked out her window to see what was happening with her cabbage plant.

The summer went by, and the woman wept and prayed. So as to hear even just a little of what was happening out on the balcony, she slept on the floor right next to the door. When there wasn't any rain, she worried that the cabbage would wilt; when there was rain, she worried that it would drown; but the mother forbade herself to think for even one second about what her little Droplet was doing there, what she was eating and how she was crying, there by herself in her green grave, without a single motherly caress, without any warmth at all . . .

Sometimes, especially at night, when the rain came down in buckets and the lightning flashed, the woman tore herself up trying not to go out on the balcony and cut down the cabbage plant and take out her little Droplet and feed her a drop of warm milk and put her into her cozy bed. Instead, she ran downstairs and stood in the rain, making quite a spectacle of herself, to show her Droplet that there was nothing scary about rain and lightning. And the whole time she told herself it must have been for a reason that she'd met the filthy hermit-monk and that he'd told her to put her little Droplet back where she found her.

In this way a summer passed, and the autumn came. All the produce stores were selling young firm cabbage plants, but the woman couldn't bring herself to go out on the balcony yet. She was afraid she wouldn't find anything there. Or she'd find a wilted cabbage plant and inside a little clump of red silk, the dress of poor Droplet, whom she'd killed with her own hands, just as she'd once killed her unborn child.

And then one morning the first snow fell, unusually early for autumn. The poor woman looked out her window, terrified, and rushed to open the door to her balcony.

As the door began to open, reluctant, with a heavy creaking sound, the woman heard a frightened meowing from the balcony, persistent and shrill.

"A cat!" the poor woman cried, thinking a cat had come over from a neighboring apartment. "There's a cat on the balcony!" And everyone knows how much cats love to eat anything that is small and runs around.

At last the balcony door opened, and the woman ran out into the snow just like that, in her slippers.

Inside her pot was an enormous, glorious cabbage, covered with numerous curly leaves like rose petals, and on top of the plant, lying on its many curls, was a thin, ugly baby, all red, with flaking skin. The baby, closing tight its tiny eye slits, made mewling noises, choking with sobs, shaking its clenched little fists, wobbling its bright-red toes the size of currant berries. And as if that weren't enough, the baby had, stuck to its bald head, a little scrap of red silk.

"But where's Droplet?" the woman thought to herself, bringing the whole cabbage plant and the baby into the room. "Where's my little girl?"

She put the crying baby on the windowsill and began digging into the cabbage. She lifted every leaf very carefully, but her Droplet wasn't there. "Who left this baby here?" she thought. "Is this a joke? What am I going to do with this thing? Look at the size of her. They took my little Droplet, and left me with this . . ."

The baby was clearly cold, its skin bluish, its cries more and more piercing.

But then the woman thought that after all it wasn't this girl-giant's fault that she'd been dumped here, and she picked her up carefully, without pressing her to her breast, took her to the bath, washed her with warm water, cleaned her off, dried her, and then wrapped her in a clean, dry towel.

She brought this new girl to her own bed and covered her up with a warm blanket. As for herself, she got her old matchbox and took out the little half-bean where her Droplet used to sleep and began kissing it, and crying over it, remembering little Droplet.

By now it was clear that her Droplet was gone. She'd been replaced by this enormous, ugly, clumsy thing with its big head and skinny arms—a real baby, and not at all hers.

The woman cried and cried, and then suddenly she stopped. She thought for a second that this other child had stopped breathing. Could it be that this girl had died, too? Oh God, could she have caught cold on the windowsill while she was digging through the cabbage plant?

But the baby was sound asleep, her eyes closed tight—a baby that no one needed, and really in fact an ugly, pitiful, helpless little baby. The woman thought there wasn't even anyone to feed it, and took her in her arms.

And suddenly she felt as if something had struck her powerfully on the breasts, from within.

And, like every mother on earth, she unbuttoned her blouse and placed the baby to her breast.

After feeding her little girl, the mother put her to bed and then poured some water into a jug and watered the cabbage plant before placing it on the windowsill.

With time the cabbage plant grew—it developed long sprouts and pale little flowers, and the little girl, when she in her turn got up on her weak skinny legs and began to walk, immediately headed over to the window, swaying, and laughed, pointing at the long, wild shoots of the cabbage-patch mom.

Marilena's Secret

THERE ONCE LIVED A WOMAN WHO WAS SO FAT, SHE COULDN'T fit in a taxi, and when going into the subway she took up the whole width of the escalator.

When sitting down, she needed three chairs, and when sleeping, two beds, and she had a job in a circus, where she lifted heavy things.

She was very unhappy—though a lot of fat people live quite happily! They are known for their kindness and sweet temper, and most of us, in general, like fat people.

But the enormous Marilena carried a secret inside her: only when she returned at night to the hotel (the circus is always traveling, after all), where, as usual, three chairs had been set up for her, and two beds—only at night could she really become herself, which is to say, two average-sized, very pretty girls, who would begin, right away, to dance.

The enormous Marilena's secret was that, once upon a time, she'd danced on the stage as two twin ballerinas, one of whom had golden blond hair, whereas the other, for variety's sake, had curls black as tar—this made it easier for the sisters' admirers to send their bouquets to the right sister.

And, naturally, a certain magician fell in love with the blonde, whereas he immediately promised to turn the second twin, the brunette, into an electric teakettle, a very loud electric teakettle, which would always travel with the married pair to remind them that this second sister, before she was a teakettle, took just one look at the magician and immediately tried to convince her sister to break off the acquaintance.

But just as he was pointing his magic wand at the brunette, her sister, the blonde, got so red in the face, and so sweaty, and irritated, and started hissing and bubbling, exactly like a teakettle in fact—that the magician realized this wasn't going to work.

"Brides like this," said the magician, who knew a thing or two about them, having been married seventeen times, "wives like this are even worse than teakettles, because whereas you can turn off a teakettle, you can't do anything about a boiling woman."

He decided to punish the troublesome twosome.

Now, all this took place in the hallway backstage, where he'd cornered the twins after the show so he could meet the blonde and propose his marriage plans right away.

It's hard to tell about his other skills—but this he certainly knew how to do.

Incidentally, if anything didn't go right for him immediately, he'd lose interest and grow bored and just abandon the whole thing halfway through.

He usually transformed his old girlfriends and wives at random into whatever came to mind: a weeping willow, or a water faucet, or a fountain in the center of town.

He liked to make them weep for the rest of their lives.

"You'll do your share of sobbing, trust me," he told the girls now, blocking them in the crowded hallway on the way to the dressing room.

"Oh, really?" answered the sisters. "And do you know that when we were born, the Fairy Butterbread said that if anyone ever makes us cry, he'll turn into a cow! And he'll be milked five times a day! And he'll spend his whole life up to his knees in manure!"

"Oh, really?" The wizard laughed. "In that case I have a present for you! You'll never be able to cry again! That's one! And two—you'll never see each other again! Now that we're at it!"

But the sisters replied:

"The Fairy Butterbread thought of that, too. She said that if anyone separates us, he'll be turned into a dysentery germ, and will spend the rest of his life in hospitals, in terrible conditions!"

"That's even better!" said the failed bridegroom-wizard. "I'll keep you two together forever and ever! You'll always be together—the Fairy Butterbread will be very pleased. Unless of course"—and here he laughed quietly to himself—"someone tries to divide you in two, in which case I agree that the guilty party should indeed be turned into a dysentery germ! I think that's fair—really your Fairy is a mensch. But who will even think of cutting you in half?"

Then the twins answered:

"That won't work! By the Fairy Butterbread's enchantment, no matter what, under any circumstances and in any weather, we need to dance together every night for two hours!"

The wizard thought about this and said:

"That's not a problem. You can have your two hours. When no one sees you, you will dance two hours every night—and you'll live to regret it, believe me."

Here the twins turned pale and threw their arms around each other and began saying their good-byes—but already they were unable to cry.

Meanwhile the wizard, chuckling to himself, waved his magic wand, and right away a girl-mountain rose up before him, pale and frightened, with a chest like a big pillow, a back like a blow-up mattress, and a stomach like a bag of potatoes.

This girl waddled heavily to the mirror, took one look, let out a groan—and fainted.

"And that's that," the wizard said sadly, and disappeared.

Why sadly? Because life always appeared to him in its worst aspects, even though he could do anything. Really, he had no life to speak of.

No one loved him, even his parents, whom he'd once, after a minor argument, turned into a pair of slippers.

Naturally his slippers were constantly getting lost.

The wizard took vengeance on everyone who failed to love him. He literally laughed at all the poor, powerless human beings, and they paid him back in fear and hatred.

He had everything: palaces, planes, and ocean liners, but no one loved him.

Maybe if some kindly soul had come along and taken care of him, he'd have brightened up, like a copper pan that has a dutiful owner.

But the trouble was that he himself couldn't love anyone, and even in the passing smile of a stranger he saw some evil scheme and a hidden wish to get something from him for nothing.

Here however we'll leave him—he walks through the wide world, not fearing anyone (which is too bad), while our fat girl was immediately kicked out of the theater by the guards, who said she had no right to be there. She wasn't even able to take the twins' purses, with their money in them— who was she to be grabbing other people's things?

Marilena—formerly Maria and Lena—nearly died of hunger in those first few days. She lived at the train station, then in the municipal gardens. She couldn't dance anymore to earn her living, and who's going to give their spare change to someone like her—who ever heard of a fat beggar?

A beggar like that needs to go away somewhere quiet and lose some weight; otherwise she'll starve.

And she'll lose that weight quickly, believe me.

But our Marilena couldn't lose weight, even if she'd stopped eating entirely: the wizard had made sure of that.

Incidentally, many overweight people seem to be cursed in just this way: no matter how much they diet, the weight comes right back, as if by black magic.

In any case, no one invited our Marilena to perform her dancing duets anymore.

First of all, because you can't dance a duet by yourself!

Second, because she was too fat.

Finally, no one recognized her, and everyone knows that you can get on in show business only if you have connections.

However, late at night in the park or among the backyards of the train station, the big fatty would turn into two very slim ballerinas and very sadly, stumbling from hunger, dance a Charleston, a tap number, some rock and roll, and the pas de deux from the ballet *Sleeping Beauty*.

But at those times no one saw her, just as the wizard had promised.

╬

Finally she figured out a way to make things better: she went to the circus and proposed a booth in which she'd eat a fried bull in ten minutes.

The directors of the circus thought this a grand idea, and they set up a trial run, in which the hungry Marilena ate an entire bull in four and a half minutes!

The bull was, truth be told, rather petite and definitely underfed, as the directors of the circus didn't want to spend too much money.

But after eating the bull, Marilena felt such a burst of strength that, in her excitement, she picked up the director and the head administrator, each with one of her pinkies, and carried them around the arena.

Here she was immediately signed up at the circus as the world's strongest woman—hailing, it was announced, from the islands of Fuji-Wuji, where she was a world champion.

No one mentioned the bull-eating anymore, as that could have incurred serious expenses.

Instead, every evening Marilena put on a show wherein she picked up a horse and buggy, a steamboat, and, as an encore, the entire first row of the audience, who sat on connected chairs.

That's the only way she could make money at the circus. In art you must always shock your audience; otherwise you'll quickly starve to death.

Breathing heavily, she'd go after every show to a restaurant, where she'd eat a whole fried lamb, drink a jug of milk, and then, without paying, take a taxi to her hotel.

Her supper was an advertisement for the restaurant— gamblers would gather there to bet on how quickly Marilena would eat her lamb.

She also went shopping in the same spirit of fun. Tailors would sew dresses for fat Marilena and then invite the television crews and photographers: Here's Marilena BEFORE, and here's Marilena AFTER. Look how she's been transformed by the dress!

And the magazines printed photos of the big happy fat girl with her pretty face—it's true that, because it was now double the size, her nose was bigger, but, on the other hand, her eyes were simply enormous, and her teeth were so big and so white that all the toothpaste and toothbrush companies threw themselves at her feet, begging her to advertise their pastes and brushes.

In other words, she became much richer than she'd ever been.

And now she became seriously annoyed by her nighttime dances, which she'd brought upon herself by making up the Fairy Butterbread when confronted by the gullible wizard.

Because by now she'd begun to forget that inside of her were two souls, and these souls kept quiet and cried without tears in the dark prison of her powerful body. In their place there grew inside Marilena's body a whole new soul, fat and gluttonous, obnoxious and fun-loving, greedy and tactless, charming when this was advantageous to her, and grim when it wasn't.

It's no secret, of course, that souls sometimes die within a person and are replaced by others—especially with age.

Marilena's new soul knew perfectly well which journalists from which papers needed to be treated to dinner before an interview, and when the best time was to visit the dance club for oppressed overweight people, and when she should deliver the companies' presents to the orphans (the companies paid her for this, too).

She no longer cared about her nightly dances or about the two souls that were allowed for some reason to appear for two hours every evening, miserable and lonely. They disrupted her entire schedule; they didn't know the way things worked, that she'd had a hard day, that there was a flight to catch at six in the morning. They didn't know how to count profit and loss, but instead would suddenly start to remember their hometown and their poor mother and father, who'd died, and this just got in the way of the whole evening's fun for Marilena.

They became especially troublesome when Marilena

acquired a fiancé, a young man named Vladimir, with very plump lips, who quickly took all her accounts upon himself, and all her calculations and negotiations.

And he became very annoyed that every evening Marilena would disappear for two hours and come back looking like a horse run ragged, and refuse to talk with anyone and turn off the phone.

He'd taken over Marilena's whole life, and he couldn't understand where these two unpaid hours were going, and he'd throw loud tantrums about it.

Marilena loved him and gave him an enormous salary, and even hired his sister Nelly. But for some reason she was too shy to tell him about those two hours.

†

One day, Nelly, the sister, announced that Vladimir had set up a vast ad campaign about dieting for Marilena. It was for two companies that specialized in diets and cosmetic operations.

And they'd be paying her an enormous sum of money!

They couldn't let this opportunity pass them by, Nelly insisted. Vladimir was off on a business trip, to both South and North America, and would return just in time to see his new, young, thin bride.

"I'll be able to dance," said Marilena—forgetting that if she became too thin the two souls inside her would die of hunger.

Nelly answered by saying that she was also going into the same clinic for some plastic surgery—she, too, would be getting younger and changing a few things about her face, she said. "So you won't suffer alone," joked Nelly, who was usually very grim.

So Marilena was taken to the clinic, where experienced surgeons photographed her from all sides, then hid these photographs for later (when they'd cause a sensation), and then led Marilena down the corridors of the clinic, farther and farther down, and finally locked her in a room—a very nice room, except it had no windows in it.

Marilena couldn't understand what was happening. She wanted to call someone, but there was no telephone. She knocked on the door, but no one came.

She started knocking harder, then simply banging on the door—and don't forget, Marilena worked as a strongwoman at the circus—but still it was in vain.

Having bloodied her hands with all her knocking, Marilena collapsed on the floor. But suddenly she heard some distant strains of music, as she always did before the dancing began, and then she saw her thin little sister, and she herself became Maria again, and together they danced.

Apparently it was time for their evening dance, and, cursing everything in the world, the two twins danced with their bloody hands.

They told each other what they'd long suspected—that this was the beginning of the end, that Vladimir had decided to get rid of Marilena and take all the money for himself, and that the clinic was a trap.

But their performance was barely over when fat Marilena devoured the dinner that had somehow appeared outside the door.

After her dinner, Marilena felt terribly sleepy and had just enough time to realize she'd been poisoned before she collapsed right where she was, next to the wardrobe.

When the prisoner awoke, she decided to fight for her life and not eat anything—she'd just drink water from the tap. But you know how fat people are—they can't go an hour without eating something—and sure enough Marilena soon had to eat what was left for her outside the door—a pot of thick meat-and-cabbage soup with the bone still in it.

After eating this she literally crashed onto the bed and lay there unconscious until she was stirred awake by the soft strains of music that announced her evening dances.

Now Maria and Lena danced together with difficulty. It was a slow, clumsy waltz, a farewell waltz, because by now it was clear: someone had decided to poison big Marilena.

For much of the time the sisters talked about their imminent death, prayed and wept without tears, bid farewell to each other, remembered their childhood, their father, who left them so early, and their mother, who died soon after.

And where their parents' souls had gone, so the sisters were now destined to go.

The next day, big Marilena didn't even have the strength to get out of bed and drink some water from the tap.

She lay there under her own enormous weight, and talked quietly to herself in her two voices—one of which was whiny and petulant, while the other was soft and kind.

"If you'd agreed to marry that wizard, none of this would have happened to us," said one voice.

"Right, and now you'd be a teakettle," said the other.

"No, we'd have convinced him not to do that! And anyway, I'd rather be living as a teakettle than dying like this."

"Don't worry," said the first soft and kind voice, "soon the angels will bring us to Mother and Father."

"We don't need anything!" wailed Marilena. "No money, no Vladimir—just let us go live somewhere on the islands of Fuji-Wuji!"

"If only," Marilena answered herself curtly.

And then a miracle occurred: with a soft rustle one of the walls slid aside, and Marilena felt the night's dampness against her skin, though she couldn't believe it.

The room slowly filled with an evening fog and the smell of jasmine and hyacinths.

The head of Marilena's bed now pushed against a wild rose bush, and its simple pink flowers hung over her pillow.

With great difficulty Marilena picked herself up, crawled into the garden, and collapsed into some stinging weeds, and a whole rain of dew fell upon her.

With her dry tongue, the thirsty Marilena licked the moisture from the grass and from her wet hands. Then she jumped up—the quiet music was already playing—and began to perform some kind of dance among the bushes, either a cricket dance, or a mosquito dance, with hops and jumps.

"Don't you see?" Maria cried out happily. "We're in heaven!"

"Oh no, already?" Lena sobbed without tears. "What about my life? Is it over?"

Just then the two ballerinas were grabbed by two sets of strong paws, and as it happens they belonged to people without any wings or white robes—just regular security guards with guns and sweaty shirts.

And the moment Lena squeaked out something like "I don't think this is heaven," they grabbed the ballerinas and dragged them along roughly, even though they didn't resist in the least bit.

The guards apparently dragged their prisoners through the wild rose bushes, because pretty soon their hands and shoulders were scratched and even bleeding, so that by the time the girls were dragged into the porter's room, they looked like a pair of wild bums.

Right away the guards wrote up a protocol about the violation of a secure zone, and then they began interrogating the sisters as harshly as they could, especially on the subject of whether the prisoners could immediately pay a fine of three million rubles. If so, they'd be released.

"Where would we get that kind of money?" the blonde Maria asked them. "We don't even know anyone here; we're just passing through. We're dancers from the ballet."

"Are you out of your minds?" the brunette Lena yelled at them. "Just grabbing people for no reason! We'll file a complaint!"

"All right—if you have no money, you're going to get a prison sentence of life without parole!" the guard said cruelly. "You don't maybe have two million? We're not greedy."

But here something strange happened. Another guard ran into the room and barked: "Who's this? This isn't her! You let her escape! What are you two doing here? Nelly's yelling like a madwoman! There's supposed to be one fat one—and you've got two ragged clothes hangers! You'll answer for this yourselves, then. She's coming now."

And sure enough, a woman all bundled up in bandages ran into the porter's room, accompanied by a suite of doctors in their robes. With all her bandages, you could recognize her only by her low, mean voice.

"What's this? Where is she? What? You want to go to back to prison? Why were you hired, huh? As soon as she escaped from her room, you kill her in self-defense! Who's this you're showing me?"

"They were just, just standing right where the wall opens," the guard defended himself. "These two rag dolls. There was no one else there."

"What, what—you crook! You dead man! Why, I'll send you to Fuji-Wuji for this! Did you forget what your sentence was? Vladimir did everything for you! He saved you from death row, and now this? What are you waiting for? Get out there and comb that garden! And put these two in separate rooms and interrogate them. Maybe they know something."

With that, Nelly and her suite of doctors left the room.

The only one left was the head guard, the one who had asked for the three million.

With a sweet smile he said: "Oh, you'll tell me everything! I have such methods—such nice methods! Oh, you'll talk, you'll confess that you killed the fat girl yourselves and ate her. And raw, at that. There's no other way. And you'll be executed! Whereas we'll be paid three million for our hard work. Marilena was supposed to be killed accidentally, anyway. Do you hear? And anyway that big fatso was all filled up with narcotics. And she was supposed to kill one of us here, by the way. That one, she looked in, she doesn't know, naturally. Telling everyone what to do. Too bad it didn't work out. But this is even easier. Oh, I have such terrible methods of torture! You'll be amazed, I guarantee you. You'd be better off confessing now, so as not to suffer too much before your execution. Because you ate her, didn't you?"

But here the two hours of dancing apparently came to an end, because Maria began to be drawn inexorably toward Lena, and Lena toward Maria, and the guard found himself in between them.

"Hey!" he yelled. "What are you doing? What's gotten into you two? I'll shoot! Stay where you are!"

Maria and Lena were already melding into each other around him.

Here the desperate guard reached behind his belt for a knife and began blindly chopping the air with it.

And right after the first blow, when he divided Maria's arm from Lena's arm, the sisters felt that they no longer needed to join together.

The bloodied, scratched-up ballerinas found themselves standing there, just staring at each other. The guard was gone.

"You know what happened?" cried the incredulous Lena. "It's just as the wizard predicted. Whoever tries to divide us will turn into a little dysentery germ!"

"Eww," said Maria, "let's get out of here! We've had enough trouble without picking up dysentery."

Shocked and staring at the floor—where, according to their calculations, right now a fat, hairy dysentery microbe should have been crawling—the sisters ran out of the room.

Sometimes one evil defeats another, and two minuses make a plus!

No one stopped them.

They ran out into the garden and stumbled around for a long time in the wet bushes until they found a gate and a guard on the lookout.

"Hurry, there's a fat woman with a knife in there! She threatened to stab us!"

"A fat one?" The guard became excited and hurled himself toward the telephone.

Lena and Maria jumped out the gate. They were free. They ran away from that cursed place as fast as they could, ran and ran, until they reached the train station, familiar from long ago.

Where else is a homeless person to go?

They washed up, first in a puddle behind some bushes (apparently it had rained in the city that night, while they were escaping) and then in the bathroom.

The few scratches on their foreheads and hands were nothing—all sorts of things can happen to wandering poor people.

At the train station, Lena and Maria looked through some newspapers that were lying around and learned that tomorrow would see the long-awaited triumphant return of big Marilena, the star of the circus, who now weighed fifty kilograms instead of one hundred.

Next to this announcement was a photo of the new Marilena (quite obviously the secretary Nelly, but with big teeth and widened eyelids, which made her look a little cross-eyed, like a bulldog—but what can you do) and an ad for a remarkable clinic where in three days a person can get a new body and also adopt a new healthy diet through the use of miraculous herbs.

It also said that Marilena was leaving the circus to pursue a new life, since she can no longer lift heavy things or eat whole lambs, and is no longer in fact the world's strongest woman nor the champion of the islands of Fuji-Wuji.

But now she's bought herself a dieting clinic and an institute for herbal remedies and appointed her husband, Vladimir, as director—they'd been married long ago, according to the paper, but kept it secret, because a great artist can't belong to just one person; she belongs to everyone.

Moreover, the new Marilena has opened a museum of the old, fat Marilena, where the fat strongwoman's old things will be displayed, including her underwear and photos of her with her husband, Vladimir.

The newspaper also printed photos of the gradual transformation of the old fat Marilena into the new Marilena, although this was obviously a fake and a cheat, as both Maria and Lena well knew. But what can't you do with photos these days!

Here, too, there was an interview with Vladimir in the

family car, a Rolls-Royce, King-Sized (the king size was made special for the old Marilena, but they couldn't just throw away a perfectly good car, could they?), in front of a new palace and in front of the very clinic the sisters had escaped from that night.

"He set everything up so well," Maria said.

"It's good we never told him about the dances!" Lena said. "That's thanks to you—you were afraid of what he'd do if he found out he had two fiancées."

They were quiet for a moment, standing in the dark train station.

"So what do we do now?" asked Lena.

"We dance," said Maria.

"Of course! Remember the old rule? In any predicament, one must dance!"

They assumed the first position and, quietly invoking the magic phrase, "one-two-three, one-two-three-four," began to perform their steps.

Immediately around them formed a small circle of bums, station workers, and sleepy late-departing passengers with their suitcases and children. Everyone clapped in delight and threw some very small coins to show their appreciation (rich people don't sit in train stations at night).

The ballerinas gathered the money quickly, knowing that wherever there's a crowd there will soon be policemen with their nightsticks, and departed from their temporary stage. They bought tickets for the next train and left this terrible town where they'd had so many adventures because of their talent and beauty.

A year later, the LenMary sisters were famous in the next town over for their wonderful dance performances in the most expensive theater, and now they were accompanied everywhere by their own bodyguard, a frail old man in a general's uniform (generals are more feared, for some reason), and they had a house on the sea and contracts to visit all the countries of the world, including the obscure islands of Fuji-Wuji.

Among their audience, incidentally, you can quite often meet the wizard, who sends them flowers, emerald crowns, and fans made from peacock feathers—he has strange tastes. He's also afraid of the sisters and their unseen protector, the Fairy Butterbread, since she was able to defeat his own powerful spell.

Now he enjoys loving from afar, in secret and out of harm's way.

Especially as the unknown and fearsome Butterbread might still punish him for his little tricks of long ago.

Strangely enough, the sisters also often receive love letters from a man named Vladimir.

He writes to say that he's loved Maria and Lena ever since he first saw them, and he doesn't even know how to choose one over the other, and so is willing to marry each of them in turn.

In the meantime, he writes, he has found himself in some financial difficulties, having been robbed by his cruel wife Marilena, who somehow put all of their shared property in her own name and then ran off to who knows where. Meanwhile the clinic that he, Vladimir, headed has been infected by dysentery, and the government forced him to burn the whole thing down! So for the time being Vladimir asks for a temporary loan of just thirty million, with a payback period of forty-nine years.

These letters are always accompanied by photos of Vladimir in his swimsuit, in a tuxedo at a fancy ball, in a turtleneck reading a book, and in a leather coat and hat next to the smoking ruins of his clinic, with a rueful smile on his pale face.

The sisters, it's true, never read these letters. They are read in his free time—and with great interest—by the old general, who then files them into a folder, affixes a number, and places it on a shelf, hoping that someday he will be able to retire and in his retirement write a novel, with photographs, about the surprising power of the love of one young man, V. *The Sorrows of Young V.,* it will be called.

The Old Monk's Testament

THERE ONCE LIVED AN OLD MONK WHO CLIMBED UP TO HIS mountain monastery with a small box of donations.

Things were not going well at the monastery, which was far away from all the roads. The monks had to fetch their water from a stream deep in the canyon, and their meals consisted of scraps of bread and dried pancakes, which they collected as donations in the godless villages nearby. The monks gathered wild fruits and nuts in the forest, as well as berries and roots, and they also looked for honey and mushrooms—they ate those, too.

It was useless, in those parts, for the monks to try to keep a vegetable garden: during harvesttime someone would come along at night with a shovel and make off with everything. Those were the ways of the area, unfortunately.

Because of this, the peasants in the nearby towns were extremely unkind to strangers and beggars. They guarded their little plots with rifles in hand, the entire family taking shifts. They buried extra vegetables underground in the basement.

The impoverished monastery, on the other hand, stood unguarded in the forest. It was a popular target for local kids who needed money for vodka. Eventually the monks learned to do with the absolute bare minimum—tin cans for boiling water in, some straw to sleep on, old sacks for blankets. As for the honey and berries, which could after all be stolen, they hid them in the forest, in the hollows of trees, like squirrels.

They used kindling for heat, since even their ax and saw had been stolen from them.

Then again, that was the monks' vow, wasn't it—to work only with what God had given them, to work only for Him, and to make do with the same food as rabbits and squirrels.

They ate neither fish nor fowl, and each day of this existence they blessed.

But they did sometimes need a little bit of money to buy candles, and oil for their homemade tin burners, and to fix the roof, for example, or to help really and truly poor people buy some medicine.

Their icons had all been stolen, so the monks painted the walls of the monastery themselves—in fact they did this so beautifully that people tried to get in and cut these paintings out of the walls. But that didn't work. You needed real museum training to extract a painting from a wall, and since when did thieves work hard and master a craft?

During winter, the monastery was freezing. There wasn't enough kindling to heat the space, and the monks refused to break branches off living trees. But cold and hunger are hardly problems for a monk—in fact they're blessings, and, what's more, during the winter months the monastery got a break from being robbed. Who's going to drag himself through the hills and snow to break into a frozen monastery—even though every morning the monks rang, not a bell, because the bell had been stolen and sold for its metal, but an iron crossbeam.

It was an ancient crossbeam—the old bell had hung from it—and the hardworking local thieves, try as they might, weren't able to bring it down.

The monks rang their crossbeam with a secret metal crowbar they had. It was the only defense they kept on hand to fend off wild animals, say, or to break through the ice for water when their stream froze, or to beat a path through the forest.

And it's not like the local thieves really cared that much about this piece of secret scrap metal—who'd want to drag it through the forest, for one thing, and for another it wouldn't fetch more than a few kopeks at the market anyway.

And so every morning the people in the surrounding villages could hear the melancholy sound of the metal crowbar against the old crossbeam. Of course no one was so stupid as to heed the call and come there for prayer.

Who calls a doctor to heal a healthy person? Who fixes what isn't broken? Why run off to pray to God when everything is fine?

Baptisms and burials—those were sacred, sure. But no one was about to knock their foreheads against the cold floor and wave their arms about—with the exception of a dozen deaf old ladies and a few God-fearing women who apparently had nothing better to do. Once in a while the monastery would also receive visitors who were in mourning—but mourning is something that passes; one day you look and the person is fine again.

But the monks themselves prayed. They prayed for the entire population of the surrounding villages, prayed that they be forgiven for their sins.

✝

The monks lived peacefully and happily, in silence, and the head monk, old Trifon, was sad only that his days were coming to an end and that there was no one to replace him. None of the other monks really wanted to be in charge—they all considered themselves unworthy, and in fact condemned the very thought of having authority over others.

Old Trifon talked to God constantly, without interruption; there was no one to distract him from this task, except during holidays.

The local population adored holidays. They'd all get together, bring wine and snacks, and come to the forest for a big party. The monks always spent a long time afterward cleaning up.

Weddings and funerals and baptisms were also traditionally held at the monastery.

But no one liked dragging themselves all the way out there, so for a long time now everyone had been talking about opening a branch of the monastery in the central village, so they could hold their wakes and marriages and baptisms at a more convenient location. They could just build a chapel, really, and that would be that.

Unfortunately, such an undertaking would require money, and spending money, especially collectively, was something the local people didn't especially like. Whenever money was collected for such projects, it would be stolen before it could be spent. So sometimes they called old Trifon into town, and he would bury someone, and baptize someone else, and then go around the village to raise a little money for the monastery.

People gave money to the old monk grudgingly, suspecting him of trying to grow rich off the work of others, as they themselves would try.

It couldn't be said that the people of the valley were doing badly. There hadn't been any wars recently, or fires, or floods, droughts, famines. The livestock multiplied, their little plots gave plentiful harvests, and their wine barrels were never empty. You might even say that prosperity had reached the valley.

On the other hand, it couldn't be said that all was well with the ways of the people. For example, they didn't like the sick, and considered them parasites. This was especially the case if the sick person was not one of their own—if it was a neighbor, say, or a distant cousin.

If the sick person was part of the family, he'd be tolerated. But medicine cost money, and the doctor also wanted to be paid . . . so for the most part they treated the sick with the ancient folk methods, drawing some blood, then off to the steam room for a good steaming. Either that or they'd just take them into the forest and leave them there. It was thought that whoever died in the forest would go straight to heaven.

The monks would visit these dying people in the forest and bring them back to the monastery if they could. But what could the monks do for them there? They'd give them some hot water with dried berries and a teaspoon of honey.

The people down below, in the villages, didn't approve of this. It was difficult for a healthy peasant to imagine that someday he too would have to lie down on the moss in the woods and wait for death.

The old monk wandered tirelessly down the roads, in the heat and cold, visiting the villages, the towns, himself small and dried out, whispering his prayer—and people would throw a bit of change into his little box.

Incidentally, beggars weren't tolerated in those parts. Instead of being given spare change, they'd be confronted with nasty questions and some useful life lessons.

But the old monk answered all the questions put to him—was he really a monk? what sort of glue did he use to keep his long beard attached? wasn't he just a gypsy in disguise? and won't he just take the money, earned with someone else's sweat and tears, to the nearest bar for a drink?—indirectly, with a prayer, or a saying, or a joke.

The local wits even followed him just to hear him answer, laughing with particular pleasure when they heard his prayer, as if this were a particularly clever way of dodging a question, and thinking maybe they should use it themselves.

The monk would sleep right there in the street, wherever he'd been collecting alms, like a homeless dog. He would stay in town a few days, and toward evening there would always be some bleeding-heart woman (there are some people you just can't do anything about) who would sneak out and hand him a little scrap of bread, or some vegetables, or even a bowl of hot porridge.

Some of them, seeing him sleeping there at night, would cover him up with a sack or some other warm thing, especially if it was raining.

Some would stay with him a while, talk about life, say a prayer.

One time his trip down to the town ended unhappily. Trifon barely received any donations in his box, and then during the night he was robbed. Two men pushed him to the ground, searched him roughly, and, when he said "God be with you," merely gave him a knock to the head. Then they left, taking his cash box.

Trifon was very sorry about the box. It had been crafted many years before by the previous head of the monastery, the saintly old Antony, just before his death.

Lying in the ditch with his head bleeding, the monk heard the two robbers turn the corner, get into an argument about who should open the box, then finally open it. The change inside spilled out, and they used a lighter to see how much there was. When they saw how little money their robbery had earned them, they came back to the monk to get at his real riches, since clearly he'd hidden them somewhere. They ripped off his robe, searched him again, and again found nothing. So then they started beating him in earnest, this time with their boots.

They didn't beat him to death, but when Trifon regained consciousness the next morning, he found that his robe was ripped to tatters and his donations box was crushed. The old monk got up, gathered the coins that even the robbers hadn't deigned to pick up, tied them in a bundle with what was left of his robe, used another strip for loincloth, and, looking that way, bloody and filthy, began walking down to the stream to clean out his wounds.

He was recognized there by the women doing their wash. They were horrified to see his wounds and took him to a kind old woman who treated him, quickly sewed him a new robe out of old sack, and told him to leave town—there was no protection for him here.

The two robbers were known all over town. They had been going around at night for a long time, robbing and killing, and no one stopped them, because one of them had a father who was a judge.

The judge had thrown his son out of the house for stealing from the family, at which point the son decided to embarrass his father by landing himself in jail, in which case the judge might well have lost his job.

But the judge didn't want to lose such a comfortable post, so he gave an order that his son's antics be ignored. It was decided that the police would not respond to the provocations—that's all they were—of this clown.

Where there's no judge, death will stalk the earth. And death had taken up residence in the town. Those who were beaten to death, whether in the street or in the famous forest, were left to die without any investigations or arrests. Everyone was afraid to search for the truth, so no one reported the robberies and beatings. In fact anyone who reported these things would himself be arrested immediately and taken off somewhere outside town.

The monk learned a great deal, lying there on the mound of straw in the kindly old woman's house. He even learned that next door there lived an inconsolable young widow whose husband had been killed one night while taking their sick baby to a doctor in the next village. The mother had been lying in bed, herself ill with fever, when apparently the husband met the frightful pair—Red and Blondie, they were called—on the road.

The sick little boy cried and screamed all night beside his father's body. He was finally found by his mother, who'd somehow managed to get up and set off for the next town herself, also to see the doctor.

Now this woman, having buried her husband, was left without any resources, and the little boy had never quite recovered, so now every day the woman sat in front of the courthouse, begging, but everyone was afraid to give her any money.

As soon as he was able to walk, the monk got up and went to the courthouse and gave this woman his tiny little bundle of coins. And in doing so he said: "Tomorrow morning the both of you are to get up and head for the monastery in the hills, following the path above the stream. I will meet you at the big rock—I will be lying on my back next to a young spruce tree. At first two young men—Red and Blondie—will be with me, and I'll be lying with a knife when you arrive. You have to stay with me for thirty days. After that your little boy will get better."

The young pauper pressed the little bundle of change to her heart and kissed the hem of the monk's coat.

†

For his part the monk began to wander around and finally found what he was looking for: a bar on the edge of town.

The two young criminals, Red and Blondie, were inside, in garish cowboy outfits, with gold chains everywhere they could fit them. All around them hovered the shadows of the people they had killed—though no one saw them except the old monk.

The shadows hovered sadly and quietly: little children, young girls in their white burial robes, with wreaths on their heads, and stooped old people—there were lots of those.

Two restless shadows of bloodied men also flitted about— they hadn't been buried yet, apparently.

The two robbers were unhappy, their faces filled with loneliness and anger: no one went out after sunset anymore, or if they did go out they traveled in groups, in entire bands practically, armed with rifles. The people around here weren't stupid. Last time the robbers went out they managed to kill only two people—a man and the doctor he was leading to his house because his wife was giving birth. When the baby was born in the morning, he was already fatherless.

The trouble was that neither the doctor nor the expectant father had any money on them, and so today the two entre-preneurs didn't have a kopek between them.

They sat and drank—they'd been served a large jug of wine.

But they knew that in daylight the people wouldn't let them leave the bar without paying—they'd start yelling, bring a crowd, beat them up if they were lucky, maybe even take all their gold chains and rings.

By the time the police arrived, it would all be over for the two cowboys.

The tension in the bar grew.

Already the bartender was surrounded by a small crowd—an enormous cook, a rude waiter holding, for some reason, an ax in his hand, and the local idiot, an unshaved kid with small eyes, big fists, and a wide smile on his face.

The local people didn't like the judge's son very much.

The monk approached the two gloomy customers and sat down at the next table.

He ordered a glass of wine and said loudly to the waiter: "Do you have change for a gold coin? I'm going to the monastery tonight with happy tidings—a parishioner has bequeathed us a pile of gold!"

The waiter wasn't a fool. He knew monks were crooks just like everyone else. They were always complaining about how poor they were, how impoverished, and yet they lived. And so the question was: what did they live on, eh?

The waiter gave the monk a glass of wine and a crooked smile and said: "No, no change. The customers haven't settled up yet."

This conversation was heard very clearly, of course, at the next table, where four ears pricked up—professionally, so to speak—and ten fingers tensed.

When the monk got up, without having touched his

wine, and limped toward the door, the waiter didn't follow him—that was done by the two who'd just drunk a free jug of wine.

"We'll pay you double tomorrow," they told the waiter.

The waiter shrugged and said: "I haven't lost my mind just yet. Leave some collateral, then you can go."

It was light out, and people were still about, and there were cars and wagons on the road. The monk was a very well-known personage in the town. People said hello to him on the street, and he'd bless people's backs as they walked by— but of course no one had time to talk about holy things with old Trifon. The whole town saw how the monk walked out, and the whole town knew that he was carrying a sackful of gold, and that it wasn't even his gold—they knew that, too. They also knew the monk was drunk, having polished off a whole jug of free wine.

And no one so much as blinked, seeing the two following the monk in broad daylight, brazenly, just ten steps behind.

Those two walked angrily, which was understandable: a waiter, swinging a butcher's ax for emphasis, had just taken a gold watch and chain from them.

The whole town also knew that those two would be back at the bar as soon as it grew dark. Whereas the monk would return to his monastery without any gold, and humiliated, with a black eye—and it was just what he deserved, too, as the town was perfectly well aware.

But things turned out differently.

Early in the morning a young woman left town with her little child on her back.

She walked ahead with determination and did not make way when she spotted two figures in cowboy outfits covered in blood.

For some reason the woman remained alive, whereas the police station soon received a visitor—the judge's son—who confessed to the murder of old Trifon the monk, and said that his friend had had nothing to do with it.

As always, no one listened to him. They grew bored and returned to their offices.

No one knew that on the road outside town the following conversation had taken place between the woman and the two killers.

Blocking her way, they'd said: "Where's a pretty young thing like you off to?"

"I'm going to meet Trifon the monk," said the woman, growing pale.

"The monk?" said the two, looking at each other.

"Yes, Monk Trifon—he's waiting for me."

"He's not waiting for you," said the first, laughing a little and then putting his hand, with blood caked under its fingernails, on her breast.

"He's waiting for me," repeated the woman, moving back and taking her child off her shoulders. "He's waiting for me on the high road above the stream, under a young spruce— he's lying there with a knife, under a big rock."

"How do you know that?" asked the first, his voice suddenly grown hollow.

"He told me that you two—Red and Blondie—would meet him by the big rock. And . . . he'd be lying there with a knife."

She suddenly realized what had happened, and continued confidently: "You were going to kill him, Trifon said, and leave the knife in his chest."

"That's exactly what he said?" the red-haired one asked, laughing nervously.

"Yes! And he told me to sit with him for thirty days, at the end of which my boy would walk again."

She placed the boy on the ground, but his legs gave way under him. He couldn't stand.

"Good-bye," said the woman, picking up her child and going on her way.

The two cowboys exchanged a glance and then went into the town without looking at each other.

Their confessions at the police station were so stubborn and determined this time that finally the detectives went up into the hills to gather evidence. But when they arrived at the scene, there was nothing there.

The only thing under the young spruce near the big rock was a small mound of dry earth, with a thin candle atop it. Three monks sat there praying alongside a woman as pale as death, holding a child. Next to them some mushrooms in a tin can cooked over a fire.

Still the two young men insisted they be put to death—they kept naming the time and place of the murder and showing their nails, which were still stained with blood.

Moreover, they named one hundred twenty-three other crimes they had committed and even took the police to the man who'd bought all their stolen goods, though he claimed not to know them. And yet he gladly invited everyone to drink a bottle from the wine cellar of his brand new home.

The two outlaws were told to go away, and they slunk out of town.

But the murders and robberies stopped.

┼

A month later, two people entered the town: a woman, and a small boy who held her by the hand. He was walking slowly, uncertainly, but nonetheless walking on his own.

The mother and her child walked through the town—and the women of the town, seeing them pass, would turn their heads toward them, like sunflowers, and remain watching like that for some time.

"He's walking," they'd say quietly.

Immediately the mothers, wives, and daughters of the sick—and there turned out to be more in the town than anyone knew—learned about the miracle that had taken place, and all of them came to see the widow, who told them all the same thing: She'd lived for a month next to the grave of the holy monk Trifon, and at the end of it she'd hung her boy's shirt on a branch of the spruce to dry, and he'd immediately stood up on his little feet.

A month before, she said, she'd taken the path above the stream to the big rock and found the monk lying there, dying, with a knife in his chest—he was holding it with his hand.

He blessed her and the boy and asked her to bring his friends from the monastery, and he bid farewell to them all and asked them to bury him right there by the rock where he lay.

He didn't say anything to the woman, but she remembered his testament, that she should live a month beside him. She was frightened that the two bandits would return, and she kept a fire going every night, for exactly one month, and then it was summer, and it was very hot, and she'd hung her boy's shirt on the spruce branch—and he'd stood up and walked.

The town was in a frenzy. They carried the boy from house to house, and entire processions set off on the path above the stream. Sick people went, and people who wanted to ask the holy monk for a husband, or for riches, or to be released from prison, or that their unpleasant neighbors receive a punishment from God.

The monks from the monastery built a chapel next to the holy grave. More and more people flocked to it, and soon the town's mayor built a hotel to house visitors from other towns, and the people began selling water from the stream. The spruce was fenced off, and admission was charged to the grave. But this didn't affect the monastery at all. The monks continued to live in poverty, eating very little, and giving everything away to the poor.

It quickly became clear that the old monk didn't help everyone—only those who were honest, virtuous, and poorly treated, and especially widows with children. But everyone went anyway, because who after all is not honest, virtuous, and poorly treated in our day and age? And what old woman is not a widow with children?

Incidentally, the number of monks at the monastery increased to seventeen. The two new monks never show their faces, just pray day and night in the upper monastery, afraid to go down to the grave by the rock, where lies the old monk whom they killed, and who saved their lives by giving up his own.

The Black Coat

THERE ONCE LIVED A GIRL WHO FOUND HERSELF IN AN unknown place, on a cold winter night. She was dressed in a strange black overcoat. Underneath the coat she was wearing a tracksuit, and on her feet some sneakers.

The girl didn't remember her name or who she was.

It was winter, and she began to feel very cold, standing there by the side of the road. There was forest all around; it was growing dark. She'd better start walking, it occurred to her—it didn't matter where—for it was getting really cold, and the black coat didn't keep her warm at all.

She began to walk down the road. Suddenly a small truck appeared. The girl signaled, and the truck pulled over. The driver opened the door. There was another passenger in the cabin.

"Which way are you headed?" asked the driver.

The girl blurted out, "And which way are you headed?"

"The train station," the driver answered with a laugh.

"Me, too," said the girl. (She remembered that people should look for a train station when they're lost in the woods.)

"Then let's get going," the driver said, still laughing.

"But there's no room for me in the cab!" said the girl.

"Of course there is. My companion is nothing but bones."

The girl climbed in, and the truck began to move. The second man made some room for her, grudgingly. His face was concealed under a hood.

They drove quickly past snowdrifts down the darkening road. The driver didn't speak but continued to grin, and the girl didn't speak either, in case they'd notice she'd lost her memory.

They drove up to a train station. As soon as the girl got out, the door slammed behind her, and the truck darted on ahead. The girl walked up to the platform, where a local train was getting ready to depart. She remembered that one needs to buy a ticket. She checked her pockets for money, but all she could find was some matches, a scrap of paper, and a key. She was too shy to ask where the train was headed. Anyway, there wasn't a single passenger on it; her compartment was empty and also poorly lit.

Finally the train stopped, and she had to get off. It was, apparently, quite a big station, but at this hour it was completely deserted, and the lights were turned off. Around the station there were traces of what seemed to be a construction site: the ground was covered with ugly black pits. There was nothing for the girl to do but walk into the tunnel under the platform. It was dark, but the tiled walls emitted a strange light, and the sloping floor was uneven. The girl raced down the tunnel, her feet barely touching the floor, like in a dream, past more black pits and some shovels and carts (probably another construction site).

The tunnel finally ended, and the girl found herself on the street, trying to catch her breath. The empty street was in ruins. The buildings were dark, some missing windows and roofs, and the street was blocked by roadwork signs and covered with potholes. The girl stood on the curb, freezing in her thin black overcoat.

Suddenly the same truck pulled over. The driver opened the door and told the girl to hop in. Sitting by the driver was the same passenger in a black hooded overcoat. He seemed to have gained some weight and now almost filled the seat.

"There's no room in here," the girl said as she climbed in. Actually, she was glad to run into the only people she knew in this unfamiliar place.

"Sure there's room," the driver laughed back, turning to face her.

And there was plenty of room, she discovered: there was even space left between her and the gloomy passenger, who turned out to be very skinny: it was his coat that took up the most room.

The girl decided she would go ahead and tell them she didn't know anything.

The driver, too, was very thin; otherwise they couldn't have made themselves so comfortable in that tiny cabin. The driver's nose was very stubby, and he was pretty ugly; he was completely bald and yet seemed very merry—he was constantly laughing, baring all his teeth. In fact, he never stopped grinning but somehow never made a sound. The other passenger kept his face hidden under his hood and was silent. The girl was silent, too: she had forgotten everything. They were passing empty streets, riddled with holes. The residents of that neighborhood must have been fast asleep in their homes.

"Where to?" asked the merry driver, showing all his teeth.

"I need to get home," replied the girl.

"And where would that be?" the driver asked, laughing noiselessly.

"Well, we should take a right at the end of this street," the girl said hesitantly.

"And after that?" the driver asked, chuckling.

"And then we'll just keep going straight."

The girl was afraid they'd ask for the exact address.

The truck was going very fast, but making no sound, even though the road was all holes.

"Where now?" asked the merry driver.

"Right here is good, thanks," said the girl, and she began to open her door.

"And who's going to pay?" the driver widened his cavern of a mouth. The girl once again searched her pockets and again found matches, a scrap of paper, and a key.

"I don't have money on me," she confessed.

"Don't accept rides if you can't pay," cackled the driver. "We didn't charge you the first time, and so you decided to make it a habit. Bring us money or we'll eat you. We're skinny and starved, isn't that right? Isn't that right, you dummy?" he addressed the other passenger with a laugh. "We feed on the likes of you! Just kidding."

They all got out of the truck together. They were in some empty lot now, sparsely strewn with new apartment buildings that appeared deserted (at least, there were no lights). Some lonely streetlamps cast light on the lifeless windows.

The girl, still hoping for something to happen, walked as far as the last building and stopped. Her companions also stopped.

"Well, is it here?" the grinning driver asked her.

"Maybe," the girl said, as if she might be joking, but she felt very awkward: in a moment they'd discover she'd forgotten everything.

They entered the building and began to walk up the dark stairs. Luckily, one could see the steps. The stairwell was very quiet. The girl chose a random floor and stopped at the first apartment, took out a key, and easily unlocked the door. The foyer was empty, and they walked through the apartment. The first room was empty too, but in the second room they discovered a tall pile of rags in the far corner.

"You see, there's no money, but you can take these things," said the girl to her guests.

She noticed, as she spoke, that the driver's mouth was still open in a grin, while the other man kept looking away, hiding his face.

"And what is all this stuff?" asked the driver.

"These are my things. Take them—I won't need them."

"You mean it?" the driver asked.

"Of course."

"Well, then," the driver said, bending over the pile. Together with the passenger he examined the pile, and they began putting some of the things into their mouths.

The girl stepped back noiselessly and tiptoed into the corridor.

"I'll be right back," she called out, seeing the two heads turn in her direction.

In the corridor she tiptoed to the door and then out onto the stairs. Her heart was pounding, and she couldn't catch her breath. "Thank God the very first door opened with my key. No one noticed that I don't remember anything," she thought.

She walked down one flight and heard loud steps behind her.

Immediately she thought of trying the key again and, to her surprise, it opened another door. She sneaked inside and locked the door behind her.

The apartment was empty and dark.

No one was pursuing the poor girl; no one was knocking at the door. Who knows, maybe the two strangers finally gave up on her and walked away with their pile of rags.

Now she could consider her situation. The apartment wasn't very cold—that was good. She'd found a shelter, finally, albeit a temporary one, and she could lie down somewhere in the corner. Her neck and spine ached with fatigue. The girl walked quietly through the apartment. The windows let in light from the street, and the rooms were completely empty. When she entered the last room, her heart began to beat faster—she noticed a pile of rags in the corner, the same corner as in the apartment upstairs.

The girl waited for something else to happen, but nothing happened, so she walked to the pile and lay down on the rags.

"Are you crazy?" She heard someone's choking voice and felt the rags moving beneath her like snakes. Immediately two heads and four arms poked through them: her two companions were vigorously making their way through the pile until, finally, they were free.

Her knees weak, the girl fled to the stairwell. Directly behind her, someone was slithering into the corridor. Then suddenly she saw a streak of light underneath the nearest door. Again, the girl used her key to unlock that apartment.

A woman stood on the doorstep, holding a burning match.

"Please," whispered the girl, "please save me."

Behind her, her two companions slithered down the stairs.

"Get in," said the woman, lifting the match.

The girl tumbled inside and shut the door.

The stairs were quiet; they must have stopped to think.

"What do you think you're doing, bursting into other people's apartments at this hour?" the woman asked her roughly.

"Please, let's get away from this door. Let's go somewhere we can talk," pleaded the girl.

"I can't, the match will die if I walk," the woman said hoarsely. "We only get ten matches each."

"I've got some right here—please, take them."

She found the matchbox in her pocket and offered it to the woman.

"Light one yourself," the woman said.

The girl lit a match, and in its flickering light they walked down the corridor.

"How many do you have?" asked the woman, glancing at the matchbox.

The girl shook the box.

"Not many," said the woman. "Now you probably have only nine left."

"Do you know how to escape?" whispered the girl.

"You can wake up, but not always. I won't wake up anymore. My matches are all gone—bye-bye," and she began to laugh, baring her large teeth. She was laughing quite noiselessly, as if she simply wanted to stretch her mouth.

"I want to wake up," said the girl. "I want to end this horrible nightmare."

"As long as your match is burning, you can escape. I've just used my last match to help you. Now I don't care what happens. In fact, I'd rather you stay. You know, it's all very simple—you don't have to breathe. You can fly wherever you want. You will need neither light nor food. The black coat will protect you from all your problems. I will soon fly over to check on my children. They were little brats—they never listened to me. The younger one spat at me when I told them their father wasn't coming back. He cried, and then he spat. I can't love them anymore. I dream of how I'll fly to look at my husband and his new girlfriend. I don't care about them, either. I've understood everything, finally. What a fool I was!"

And she laughed again. "With the last match my memory came back. I've remembered my entire life and know I was wrong. Now all I can do is laugh at myself."

Indeed, she was grinning widely and soundlessly.

"Where are we?" asked the girl.

"I can't tell you, but soon you'll find out. There will be a smell."

"Who am I?"

"You'll find that out, too."

"When?"

"When the last match is gone."

The girl's match had almost burned down.

"While it's burning you can still wake up. I don't know how. I couldn't."

"What's your name?"

"Soon they will write my name with black paint on a small metal plaque that they will stick into a pile of dirt. When I read it, I'll find out. A can of paint has been opened; the plaque is ready, too. Others don't know yet—neither my husband, nor his new girl, nor the children. It's so empty here! Soon I'll fly away. I'll see myself from above."

"Please don't go," pleaded the girl. "Do you want some of my matches?"

The woman thought and said, "I suppose I could take one. I think my children may still love me. They're going to cry. No one wants them—their father with his new wife doesn't want them."

The girl stuck her free hand into her pocket and pulled out not the matchbox but a scrap of paper.

"Listen to what it says! 'Please don't blame anyone. Mother, forgive me.' A moment ago it was blank!"

"Aha, so that's what you wrote on yours. Mine said, 'Can't go on like this. Children, I love you.' Just now the words appeared."

And the woman pulled out her note from the black coat's pocket. She began to read it and suddenly exclaimed: "Look, the letters are disappearing! Somebody must be reading it. Someone has already found it. . . . The 'c,' the 'a' are gone, the 'n' is disappearing, too!"

The girl asked her, "Do you know why we're here?"

"I do, but I won't tell you—you will find out yourself. You still have a few matches left."

The girl took the matchbox and offered it to the woman: "Take them! Take them all! But please tell me."

The woman divided the matches and asked, "Do you remember who the note was for?"

"No."

"Then light another match—this one is out. With each match I remembered more."

So the girl took out her remaining matches and lit all four of them.

Everything became illuminated: she could see herself standing on a chair; on the desk she could see the note that said "please don't blame anyone"; outside the window lay the dark city, and her lover, her betrothed, wouldn't pick up the phone after she'd told him about her pregnancy; instead his mother would answer, "Who is it and what do you want?"—knowing perfectly well who it was and what she wanted.

The last match was burning down, but the girl wanted to know who was sleeping in the next room, who was moaning and breathing heavily as she stood on that chair, tying her thin scarf to the pipe under the ceiling. Who was that person sleeping in the next room, and the other one, who was lying awake, staring into space, crying?

Who were they?

The match was almost out.

A little longer—and the girl knew everything.

And then, in that empty, dark apartment, she reached for her scrap of paper and lit it with the dying match.

And she saw that on the other side, in the other life, in the next room her ailing grandfather was asleep, and her mother was on a cot by his side because he was dangerously ill and constantly needed water.

And someone else, someone who loved her and whose presence she could sense was there too—but the note was burning so quickly—that someone was standing in front of her, offering her consolation, but she could neither see nor hear him, her heart was too full of pain. She loved only her betrothed, him and only him; she no longer loved her mother or her grandfather, or him, who was offering her consolation that night.

Then, at the very last moment, when the little flame was licking her fingers, she felt the desire to speak to him. But the poor little scrap of paper was burning out, as were the last fragments of her life in that room with a chair. And then the girl pulled off the black coat and touched its dry fabric with the last flame of her note.

Something snapped. She smelled burning flesh, and two voices outside shrieked in pain.

"Take off your coat now!" she cried to the woman, who was smiling peacefully, her mouth stretched wide open, the last match dying in her hand. And the girl, who was still here, in the dark corridor with the smoking overcoat, but also in her room perched on a chair, gazing into those loving eyes—she touched the woman's coat with her burning sleeve, and immediately a new double howl was heard from the stairs. A revolting smoke came from the woman's coat, and the woman threw off the coat and immediately vanished.

The room around her vanished, too.

That same moment the girl stood on a chair with a scarf tied around her neck and, choking with saliva, was looking at the note on the desk, fiery circles dancing before her eyes.

In the next room someone groaned, and she heard her mother asking sleepily, "Father, want some water?"

As quickly as she could, the girl untied the scarf and took a breath; with shaking fingers she loosened the knot on the pipe, jumped off the chair, crumpled the note, and flopped on her bed, pulling the covers over her.

Just in time.

Her mother, blinking from the light, peeked into the room. "Dear God, what a terrible dream I've just had: a pile of earth in the corner, and from it some roots were growing . . . and your hand," she said tearfully. "And it was stretching toward me, as if asking for help . . . Why are you sleeping with your scarf on? Is your throat sore? Let me cover you up, my little one. I was crying in my dream . . ."

"*Mom*," the girl replied in her usual voice, "you and your dreams. Can't you leave me alone? It's three in the morning, for your information!"

On the other side of the city a woman vomited up a handful of pills and washed her mouth thoroughly.

Then she went to the nursery where her fairly large children, ten and twelve years old, were sleeping, and rearranged their blankets.

Then she got down on her knees and prayed to be forgiven.

THE GIRL FROM THE METROPOL HOTEL

Growing Up in Communist Russia

Ludmilla Petrushevskaya grew up in a family of Bolshevik intellectuals who were reduced in the wake of the Russian Revolution to waiting in bread lines. In her prizewinning memoir, she recounts her childhood of deprivation—of wandering the streets and living by her wits like Oliver Twist.

THERE ONCE LIVED A MOTHER WHO LOVED HER CHILDREN, UNTIL THEY MOVED BACK IN

Three Novellas About Family

Among Petrushevskaya's most famous and controversial works, the three novellas presented here are modern classics that breathe new life into Tolstoy's dictum, "All happy families are alike; every unhappy family is unhappy in its own way."

THERE ONCE LIVED A GIRL WHO SEDUCED HER SISTER'S HUSBAND, AND HE HANGED HIMSELF

Love Stories

By turns sly and sweet, burlesque and heartbreaking, these realist fables of women looking for love are the stories that Ludmilla Petrushevskaya—who has been compared to Chekhov, Tolstoy, and even Stephen King—is best known for in Russia.

Ⓟ PENGUIN BOOKS

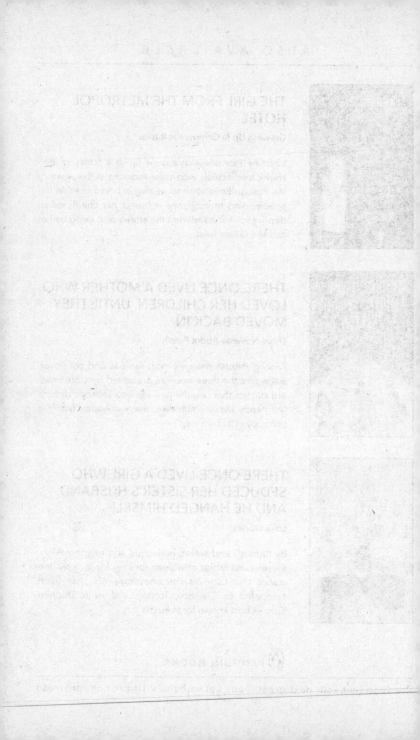